"Looks deep. Let me."

He raised his eyebrows, seeking permission to proceed. She pressed her palm more snugly into his lips, silently accepting his aid.

Travis's lips brushed her palm again in what felt suspiciously like a kiss. Seconds later he had the offending sliver of wood displayed on the tip of his finger.

"Got it." His voice had dropped another octave. The whirlpools in his eyes deepened, churning up the same emotion raging through Lindy's system.

Desire.

Standing before him, her own lips covering the same spot his had just vacated, Lindy searched her mind for a proper response. After all, proximity and convenience aside, Travis had no real interest in her.

In a few months, he'd return to his world.

She had to make sure her heart didn't go with him.

Dear Reader,

"If I'd known then what I know now."

What a concept. A chance to tackle yesterday's mistakes with today's wisdom.

The ultimate fantasy? Maybe—at least until my eleven-year-old sons perfect their time machine☺— but for Lindy and Travis Monroe, the fantasy becomes reality.

Their marriage started off rocky, more heat than heart, and when fate tested them, they fell apart. Now, thanks to the unorthodox terms of Lindy's grandfather's will, the estranged couple have been granted a do-over. Will they be smart enough to do things right the second time around?

Not right off the bat, of course. A writer's got to have her fun, after all.

I hope you enjoy Travis and Lindy's story. And remember, second chances are rare, so make the most of your life the first time around.

Wishing you laughter and love,

Dawn

TO HAVE AND TO HOLD

DAWN TEMPLE

SPECIAL EDITION®

Published by Silhouette Books
America's Publisher of Contemporary Romance

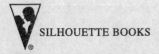

SILHOUETTE BOOKS

ISBN-13: 978-0-373-24860-5
ISBN-10:   0-373-24860-1

TO HAVE AND TO HOLD

Books by Dawn Temple

Silhouette Special Edition

To Have and To Hold #1860

DAWN TEMPLE

was born in Louisiana, and despite having now lived more than half her life in Texas, in her heart, she still considers the Bayou State home. Everything about the South appeals to her: lazy days, nosy neighbors, old buildings and ancient trees. But the best thing is the people. In fact, her favorite part of writing is trying to honestly and emotionally capture that warm Southern spirit on the page. She loves to hear readers say they really connected with one of her characters—especially among the eclectic cast she uses to populate the background. Look closely. With any luck, you might recognize a few characters from your own life.

Dawn lives in the Texas Gulf Coast region with her husband, twin sons and three neurotic dogs. Stop by for a bit of Southern hospitality at www.dawntemple.com where friends are always welcome.

Infinite thanks and love to Sandra K. Moore,
Ann Peake and Sandy Thomas for teaching me
the true meaning of conflict.

To my guys, Doug, Jacob and Jeremy. Thanks for
the underwear dance. *I* am so proud of *you.*

Chapter One

A soft purple glow drew Lindy Lewis Monroe from the solitude of the barn's dark interior. She slipped outside the wide double doors and stopped suddenly, awestruck. Before her, dawn painted the East Tennessee sky with hope and renewal, a visible reminder that life goes on.

Beautiful day for a funeral, huh, Pops?

She had a ton of things to do before burying her grandfather this afternoon, yet she stood in the barnyard for several minutes, watching the sun break over the horizon, sharing a final sunrise with the one person who'd always been there for her.

"Goodbye, Pops. I love you." Her raspy voice gave testament to the buckets of tears she'd cried during the past few days.

A chilly spring breeze drifted across the barnyard.

Goose bumps spread over Lindy's skin beneath her dew-dampened clothes. Her teeth chattered, disturbing the barnyard's unusual tomblike silence.

Quit standing around like a bump on a log, Lindy girl.

Pops's gentle reminder whispered through her brain, part memory, part wishful thinking.

Heeding her grandfather's advice, Lindy turned her back on the glorious sunrise and hotfooted it to the house. Thanks to mid-April's near-freezing overnight temperatures, her damp jeans grew colder and stiffer with every step.

The screen door squeaked as she entered the mudroom and toed off her boots, then quickly freed the button on her jeans, shimmying her lower half until the clingy, wet denim peeled from her hips.

The damp tails of her oversize shirt slapped against her bare thighs, causing more gooseflesh. She removed Pops's old red-and-black checkered work shirt and lifted it to her nose. His Old Spice scent still clung to the soft flannel. She hated the idea of laundering away that familiar smell.

Burying her face in the fabric, she wiped away a tear and let the shirt fall to the floor. Cold air enveloped her arms. She shuddered. Her T-shirt, which she'd pulled on without a bra, offered little coverage. Or warmth.

Leaving her wet clothes heaped on the floor, she stepped into the kitchen and paused for a heartbeat, letting the familiar warmth surround her, that blanket of welcome that engulfed her every time she stepped foot inside her childhood home. All her life, she'd dreamed of sharing that warmth with a family of her very own.

Not all dreams come true. She'd taken her shot at happily-ever-after and lost everything: her husband, her baby, her heart. Never again would she trust her dreams to someone else.

Don't rehash the past. Focus on today. She inhaled deeply, a cleansing breath to wash away her maudlin thoughts. The welcome aroma of her favorite Colombian brew filled her senses.

Should've known Alice would show up this morning.

Alice Robertson had been friend, neighbor and part-time housekeeper to the Lewis family for more years than anyone cared to remember. Having her here, today of all days, felt right, Lindy thought, heading for the coffeepot. A mug pre-filled with half-and-half waited on the countertop.

Such a sweet woman. For the first time since leaving the hospital three nights ago, Lindy's lips curled into a half-hearted smile. Wondering why Alice hadn't stuck around for coffee, she turned away from the cabinet and came face-to-face with the past she'd just been trying to forget.

Travis Monroe.

Her breath backed up in her throat. She clamped her eyes shut, waited a long second, then slowly reopened them. He hadn't moved a muscle.

The man she hadn't seen in almost a year leaned against the doorjamb, steaming cup in hand. His thick black hair was ruffled, no doubt from his own agitated fingers. Dark stubble covered his angled jaw. His Brooks Brothers suit was wrinkled. He looked haggard. And fantastic.

His eyes, a sexy starburst of green and gold, were riveted to the thin cotton clinging to her breasts.

Oh, great. Travis shows up unexpectedly, and I'm parading around the kitchen in my undies.

Despite her near nakedness, Lindy refused to cross her

arms in some virginal attempt to cover what he already had intimate knowledge of. "What are *you* doing here?"

Her abruptness seemed to snap him out of his stunned stupor. His eyes lifted to her face. The desire and anger she saw there made her take a step backward.

"What happened to your legendary Southern charm?"

Her chin tilted up a notch. "Manners are for friends and invited guests. *You* are neither."

"No, I'm just your husband." Travis pushed away from the doorway that separated the kitchen from the family room. His firm lips fell into a frown. She knew how warm and soft they'd feel pressed against her own.

Don't go there.

"How'd you get in here?" Surely Alice hadn't let Lindy's estranged husband in and then left without warning her.

"Your front door was unlocked."

Unlocked? She wrinkled her brow, momentarily puzzled until her brain connected all the dots. Pops had always taken care of locking up at night. Another sad twinge plucked her heart, but she determinedly tucked her grief deep inside. Later, when she was alone, she'd let it out and allow her tears to flow.

Right now, she propped her hands on her hips, pretending she wore her favorite denim overalls rather than see-through cotton. "For the most part, the only doors we lock in Land's Cross are on the henhouse. That's generally the place we have problems with unwanted varmints."

Travis's knuckles whitened against his coffee mug. "Sounds like a great slogan for the chamber of commerce."

A shameful heat warmed her cheeks. Why was it so

easy to shuck her normal kindness and stoop to rudeness with Travis?

She knew the answer to that one. Because no one else had ever hurt her like he had.

"I'll be sure to pass your suggestion along. Coming from such a career-driven person, I'm sure the chamber will give it all the attention it deserves."

"I see your tongue's as razor sharp as ever." Still standing in the doorway, he lifted his coffee and took a slow sip. Over the mug, his eyes captivated hers. "Although, I remember times when your only response was a purr. Or a moan."

Heaven help her, she also remembered those times. Remembered them too well. Too often. But that was her own dark secret. Travis didn't need to know how often he played the starring role in her memories, both during daylight hours and dark.

"I hate to disappoint you, Travis, seeing as how you've come all this way to stroll down memory lane, but my schedule's pretty tight today. And we both know what a busy man you are. Why don't I give your secretary a call later? Perhaps Marge can squeeze me in between your more important commitments."

He stepped toward her, all desire gone from his eyes. "You think I want to be here?" The muscle in his clenched jaw jumped.

"Then why are you? I didn't ask you to come."

"No, you sure didn't," he said bitterly. "You've made it clear where your loyalties lie."

A rusty sound erupted from her throat. "*My* loyalties!" Her hands began to shake, making her wish for pockets to hide them in. Why hadn't she waited to take off Pops's huge shirt? She felt as vulnerable on the outside as she did on the inside.

"You're one to talk about loyalties." How many times had Travis rushed off to rescue his "real" family, often not bothering to tell her where he'd gone or when he'd return?

"*You're* the one who ran off." Travis's voice was colder and tighter than the jeans she'd left crumpled on the mudroom floor. "Until I read that damned note you left, I never pegged you for a coward. You always bragged about being 'strong Lewis stock.'"

Strong Lewis stock. That had been Pops's motto, his answer to all life's problems.

"How dare you throw my grandfather's words in my face!" She kneaded her fist against the ache in the pit of her stomach. "You must be spending too much time with your brother. That's the kind of cruel remark I'd expect from Grant."

Hurt flickered across his features. Lindy hardened her heart. She wouldn't let her softer emotions distract her. "You obviously came here to upset me. You've succeeded. Now you can leave."

"Leave?" Travis spit the word out. "Is that your only answer? When things get sticky, pack up and crawl home."

"What choice did I have? Did you ever give me a reason to stay?" Lindy's voice rose, but she didn't care. She couldn't keep her feelings bottled up any longer. "You worked twenty hours a day, seven days a week. On the rare occasions you came home, it was just for a quick nap—in the guest room for God's sake. Do you have any idea how demoralizing that was for me? Being tied to a man who'd rather fold himself onto a bed too short and too narrow to be the slightest bit comfortable than share a king-size bed with me?"

She paused, sucking air deep into her burning lungs. Even a year later, the idea of being no more than an obligation to Travis caused her heart to spasm.

He straightened from the door frame. "I never meant to hurt you. I didn't know what you wanted. What you needed."

"You could've asked." She'd desperately needed words of comfort from him. All she'd gotten was his silence. His absence.

"I figured I had time. I wanted to wait until you'd fully recovered before—" His shoulder shrugged. "Before I broached such a sensitive subject. Our relationship was rocky enough."

"What little relationship we had died that night." Her voice hitched, as it always did when she remembered the car crash that had wrecked their lives. Her hands again covered her stomach. If their son hadn't died, would their marriage have survived?

This time, Travis's hurt was more than a flicker. It was a beacon. She'd never doubted the sincerity of Travis's grief. Unfortunately it was their only common emotion.

"I'd give anything to change what happened," Travis whispered, the warm timbre of his voice washing over her raw nerves, once more weakening her resolve.

In self-defense, she resorted to rudeness. "Well, not even you can fix the past. And I have a funeral to attend today."

She turned to leave, desperate to escape before the tears burning her eyelids broke free.

Travis's warm touch halted her getaway, his thumb gently stroking the tender flesh just south of her underarm. "I was sorry to hear about Lionel. I know how much he meant to you."

She knew the tingles coursing through her were wrong. For goodness' sake, in a few hours she would bury the only real family she'd ever had. So why did Travis's touch feel so right?

She looked pointedly to where his tanned flesh intersected with her pale skin. Knowing he couldn't miss the skip in her pulse, she played her reaction as anger, lifting her gaze to his and arching her brow.

The left side of his mouth twitched slightly. He wasn't fooled. Whatever problems she and Travis may have had, chemistry was never one of them. Every time they came within five feet of each other, they spontaneously combusted.

Lindy sighed sadly and tugged her arm free. More than anything, that explosive attraction explained how they had ended up in this mess.

"Do us both a favor, Travis. Go back to Atlanta where you belong."

Travis stood under the shade of the oak tree centered in the rural cemetery and studied Lindy from behind the protection of his sunglasses. She stood as rigid as a soldier, looking strong and composed. But her hands, wrapped in a death grip around a handkerchief, trembled.

If she doesn't bend soon, she's gonna break.

Even with an iron rod down her back and that damned chin of hers aimed to the heavens, she looked stunning. She'd tamed her blond curls into a sophisticated little knot resting on her nape. A classy black suit hugged her body, showcasing the fullness of her breasts, the curve of her hips.

She wore no sunglasses, facing the sun's glare and the crowd's speculation directly. Purple smudges tinted the skin under her blue eyes and lines formed around her tightly clenched lips. Even her nostrils flared at regulated intervals.

Against his chest, Travis's cell phone vibrated for the third time in half an hour. He slipped his hand into his suit jacket and turned it off. Monroe Enterprises, more specifically, his brother and father, would have to get along without him for a couple of days.

He wasn't going anywhere until he figured out what was going on here, why he'd been summoned to Lionel Lewis's funeral. Not that he wasn't sad to hear about Lionel's passing. They may not have seen eye to eye where Lindy was concerned, but Travis had respected the old man. In fact, he admired the way Pops had always put his family's happiness—Lindy's happiness—first.

"Let us not focus solely on our loss," the minister said. "Rather, let us remember the joy Lionel brought into our lives."

The words buzzed into Travis's consciousness, but his gaze remained focused across the crowd of mourners, where Lindy stood beside her grandfather's flower-draped casket.

His eyes flicked to the hulking Jethro reject hovering at her elbow. He recognized the bastard. He'd never forget the image of his wife's arms wrapped around this overgrown hick.

After reading Lindy's Dear John note last year, he'd raced to Tennessee to lay it all on the line, and what did he find? Lindy dancing the night away in the town square with some farm boy. Travis had stormed out of town without learning the man's name. Once back in Atlanta, he spent the evening spilling his guts to Jack Daniel's.

He knew the man's name now. The old lady who ran the

boardinghouse that passed for a hotel in this one-horse town happily supplied the man's identity over lunch.

"Thank goodness for Danny Robertson," she'd cooed. "Lindy needs a strong man to lean on during these hard times. And Danny's such a great boy."

His hostess, diligently thorough in her gossip, spared no detail about Lindy's longtime "friendship" with the CEO of the local Feed and Seed.

How can these people stand to live in this fishbowl?

Around him, the funeral crowd began reciting a hushed version of the Lord's Prayer. "Lead us not into temptation—"

Temptation. Yeah, right.

Shifting under the heat of the sun—and his rising anger—Travis watched Lindy mutilate her handkerchief. Was it possible she didn't know her attorney had called him yesterday, giving him all the details of Lionel's funeral as well as the meeting scheduled for tomorrow afternoon?

She'd seemed genuinely surprised by his presence this morning. And not just because he'd caught her practically naked. Coming face-to-face with a barely dressed, *smiling* Lindy had thrown him for quite a loop. But even through his own surprise, he'd noted the shock on her face.

The seductive vision of his wife wearing nothing but two strips of white cotton filled his brain. He couldn't remember the last time he'd seen so much of her creamy-white skin.

It had been even longer since he'd seen her smile.

His focus had been so riveted on Lindy, he didn't notice Robertson move closer to her side until the grizzly-size man lifted a paw and rested it on her shoulder.

Travis waited for Lindy's shoulder to shrug, knock the paw off, refuse the man's affection. Instead her hand lifted, touched the fingers resting on her shoulder. She craned her head, relaxed her lips, favoring him with a small smile.

The big man seemed to swell under Lindy's attention. Travis's stomach twisted, along with every other muscle in his body.

Fists clenched, he stepped forward.

Luckily common sense prevailed. He couldn't very well strike the man at Lionel's funeral. Forcing his muscles to relax, he fell back in line and tried to pay attention to the service.

Lindy smiled and greeted well-wishers until her cheeks ached. Unshed tears burned the backs of her eyes. Seemed like the entire population of Land's Cross had shown up to pay their respects.

Guilt washed over her. So many people, most she'd known her entire life. Yet all afternoon, one guest had monopolized her thoughts. Travis.

Why was he here? She'd give anything to find out he'd come to support her, to finally be there in her time of need. Her pride and her memory squashed that thought.

Would the frivolous hope lurking inside her ever accept the truth? During their brief marriage, Travis had shown over and over again that she was not his number one priority. Heck, as his wife and the future mother of his child, she hadn't even rated second best. She'd come a distant third. Far, far behind his family and his precious Monroe Enterprises.

Whatever his reasons for being here, they certainly had nothing to do with comforting her.

Since most of the mourners had already headed to the farm, she dropped her forced smile. Gritting her teeth, she watched Travis stride confidently across the grassy cemetery. He'd removed his sunglasses. His incredible eyes locked on to her, keeping her in his sights, never sparing a glance for the people or grave markers littering his path. He maneuvered through the obstacles without faltering, with the accuracy of a heat-seeking missile, she his target.

A shudder quaked through her, from the inside out.

Beside her, Danny touched her shoulder and bent close to her ear.

"You hanging in there?" he whispered.

They'd been friends since their diaper years, and she knew what he really meant. *Let me know if you need to cry and I'll carry you out of here so quick no one will see a single tear.* Danny had always been good as gold.

She managed a silent nod in answer to his question, but her gaze remained glued to Travis. He continued his approach, seemingly in slow motion. She pressed her right hand against her breastbone and forced a ragged breath into her lungs. A good twenty feet separated them. Still, Lindy felt blanketed by the pure physical force of his presence.

It was a new sensation. More than chemistry. Almost like—

Her thoughts broke when Travis cocked his head to the left, releasing her from his visual grip. Noticing movement in her periphery, her eyes rotated, blinked several times. She'd been so wrapped up in Travis, she'd forgotten where she was.

Her focus now shifted to the man who stood before her. Chester Warfield studied her, his pale blue eyes narrowed against the afternoon sun. Chester had been Pops's best friend for more than sixty years, his attorney for almost fifty. Tears filled her eyes and her tense lips quivered into a weak smile.

The stout man answered with a solemn nod and spread his arms wide. She didn't hesitate, just buried herself in his hug. His familiar scent of lemon drops and arthritis rub engulfed her. For a split second, Lindy allowed herself to pretend everything would be okay.

Then Travis cleared his throat.

Who was she kidding? Her life would never be okay again.

After a few more pats on her back, Chester released her and turned to face Travis, extending his right hand. "You must be Mr. Monroe. I'm Chester Warfield. We spoke yesterday?"

Travis dipped his head slightly in acknowledgment and accepted the older man's hand.

"Good to finally meet you in person, Mr. Monroe, even under such sad circumstances."

Lindy studied both men, Travis with his veiled expression, Chester with his odd smile. "You two know each other?"

"Not exactly." Chester's gaze settled somewhere near her earring. The tiny hairs on the back of Lindy's neck snapped to attention.

Chester cleared his throat before continuing. "As your attorney, it was my legal obligation to contact him."

Lindy shook her head, trying to make sense of Chester's words. Danny's body brushed against hers as his large hand cupped her elbow. She'd forgotten he was there.

"You ready to go?" he asked softly.

"No," she answered, stepping away from Danny's grasp. "Back up, Chester. What do you mean, 'legal obligation'?"

Lindy felt a moment's panic when Chester's face flushed and his finger dug into the neckband of his shirt. Pops's face had turned that same shade of purple moments before his heart attack.

But upon closer inspection, she realized Chester wasn't having a heart attack. Rather, he suffered from an acute case of "you're not going to like what I have to say."

Lindy's internal warning siren began to hum. Her gaze snapped back to Travis. His face gave no hint of his thoughts.

She returned her attention to her perspiring lawyer. Her finger poked the center of his chest hard enough to force him back a step. "Spill it."

Chester's eyes flicked to Danny. "This is a family matter."

What a crock.

Lindy recognized the old man's stall tactic. Still, even though Danny was practically family, a little privacy sounded like a very good idea. Fewer witnesses.

"Danny, would you mind excusing us?"

"Sure. I'll just wait by the truck and take you home when you're done."

"That won't be necessary." Travis spoke for the first time. "After the *family* details are dealt with, I'll see my wife home."

Family? Oh, great. *Now* he gets it.

Stunned, she twisted her head whiplash-fast, but the scathing comment she'd planned dissolved on the tip of her tongue. Travis and Danny stood there, less than two feet apart, shoulders thrown back, eyes squinted, sneering at each other.

Lindy stomped her foot on the ground, the way she would if her prized Holsteins Thelma and Louise were being bullheaded and needed a distraction. The heel of her black pump burrowed into the ground. *Darn it.*

"You two look like a couple of puffed-up peacocks. Cut it out!" She took a deep breath, counted to ten. Then twenty.

"Danny, I'll call you tomorrow. Okay?" She lifted her cheek to accept his kiss. With a last glare at Travis, Danny turned and headed back to his truck.

Too tired for more stalling, she addressed her attorney. "I'm assuming whatever you don't want to tell me has something to do with him." She indicated Travis with a jerk of her thumb.

Chester nodded.

"Okay." Another deep breath. "Let's hear it."

"Yesterday, I contacted Mr. Monroe in my capacity as executor of the Lewis estate," Chester said, sounding very lawyerly. "I informed him of Mr. Lewis's death and requested his presence at the reading of Lionel's will."

"Why?" Lindy's voice echoed inside her head, as if it came from the end of a very long, very dark tunnel. Her internal warning siren no longer hummed. It clanged. At full volume.

"Your grandfather left his entire estate to Mr. *and* Mrs. Travis Monroe."

The clanging in Lindy's brain stopped, replaced by the rushing roar of shock. Her heart sank to her feet, taking her blood supply with it. Despite the afternoon sun's warmth, a chill seeped into her bones. She wrapped her arms around her body and squeezed her eyes shut tight. Keeping her tears locked up felt like an impossible task.

Mr. and Mrs. Travis Monroe. The words danced a teasing jig around her brain. Suddenly the ground beneath her feet seemed to shift, throwing Lindy off balance. Travis's strong grip on her shoulders steadied the ground, righted the world.

"No," she whispered. Her eyes popped open. Travis's face hovered a few inches from hers. "Don't touch me."

She jerked her shoulders free from his hold and moved away. He stepped closer, his startled eyes drilling into hers.

"At least now I know why you're here." She widened the gap between them. This time, he didn't follow. "You came to Land's Cross because of Pops's will."

A pink tinge crept up Travis's neck, but he kept his eyes level with hers. "'Fraid so."

She'd known his reasons for being here had nothing to do with her, but hearing him admit the truth still stung. *See, Pops, he doesn't want me.*

Apparently, though, he wanted her farm. Why else would he be interested in Pops's will? Her dreams for the future were tied to that land. No way she'd let him get his hands on her dreams. Not again.

How do you know what he wants, Lindy girl? Did you ask? Did you ever tell him what you wanted? Pops's words drifted into her memory. Her old-fashioned grandfather had spent the past year trying to convince Lindy to give her marriage a second chance.

"Now, Lindy, give the boy a break." Chester's voice shocked her. For the second time in under an hour, Travis had made her forget where she was. "He's just doing what Lionel wanted."

"What about what I want?" she demanded.

Travis stepped up again and opened his mouth. Before he could speak, she raised her hand between them. "Don't bother asking, Travis. You can't give me what I want."

She wanted Pops to be alive.

She wanted to make her dream of opening Country Daze, a hands-on teaching farm for schoolchildren, a reality.

She wanted to be a wife and mother.

"I want to go home."

Travis watched Lindy stalk away, disappearing behind the giant oak in the cemetery's center. At least six feet wide, the tree hid her completely, offering the perfect place for a good cry. And if anyone deserved to shed a few tears, it was Lindy.

Knowing an audience would only embarrass her, Travis stayed put, letting her grieve in private.

You can't give me what I want.

Nothing new there. He'd failed his wife in every way possible.

Much sooner than he expected, Lindy stepped back around the tree. Her face showed no signs of a crying jag, just pure determination. Blond curls, freed from their knot, bounced on her shoulders. Bare legs protruded from the black skirt still partially bunched up around her hips. After three steps, the lightweight material resettled at her knees. Black pumps dangled from her right hand. Dark stockings hung from her left.

What the devil is she up to?

As she walked toward him, the breeze stirred. A strand of hair brushed her cheek, clung to the corner of her mouth. The black silk stockings she carried fanned out, wrapping around her derriere.

He swallowed. Hard. The lump in his throat slid into his gut. An acidic trail of need burned through him.

Beside him, Warfield expelled a forced cough.

Travis cleared his throat, dried his palms on his thighs before jutting a hand into her path. "Lindy, what're you doing?"

Without breaking her stride, she walked around his arm. "I told you. I'm going home."

He spun, watching her hips twitch as she stalked toward the road. Those sexy stockings billowed behind her, taunting him.

Warfield clucked like a little old lady.

"What?" Travis snapped.

"Nothing." Chester shrugged, smiling. Travis hated that smile, like the old guy knew a secret. "Those Lewises are the most stubborn creatures God ever put on this Earth." With a final cluck, Warfield turned and headed in the opposite direction Lindy had taken.

"Damn, these people are all nuts." Shaking his head, Travis jogged after Lindy, catching up to her quickly. He grasped her arm just long enough to stop her momentum.

"Lindy, wait. My car's this way." Pointing in the direction Warfield had gone, he indicated his silver BMW. "Come on. I'll drive you home."

She ignored him and silently resumed her escape, stomping down the road that led to the main highway. Catching up to her again, he grabbed her arm, stopping her, but this time, he didn't drop his hold. "Damn it, Lindy. I'm the only one left to give you a ride home."

She stilled, her face angled over her shoulder, her blue eyes wide as saucers in her unexpectedly pale face. For a second, she looked more scared than angry. Then her eyes narrowed. "I have no intention of taking a ride from you." Her voice quivered as she yanked her arm out of his grasp.

"Then how do you plan on getting home?"

"Walk."

"You can't walk home from here."

"Sure I can. It's only two miles." Angry color refilled her cheeks as she once more turned her back on him.

He watched in amazement as she took off again, this time cutting across the grassy lawn. The rattle of a diesel engine sounded behind Travis. He stepped to the shoulder as Warfield's truck rolled to a stop next to him.

"Told you she was stubborn, boy. She decides she's gonna walk, you can bet your bottom dollar she'll walk all the way. Leastways, she's sure not gonna take a ride from the enemy."

"Enemy?"

"You and me, boy. I know how that girl's mind works. Right about now, she figures we're in cahoots, trying to take the farm from her. Till she figures out different, I'd steer clear if I were you. Besides, Lindy'll never get in that fancy car of yours."

Travis's brow inched up. "Why's that?"

"On account of her panic attacks, of course. She barely tolerates pickups. Gettin' in a regular car's totally out of the question." Warfield lifted a cell phone and dialed, his lips turning up in a calculating smile. "I'll call Danny Robertson. He drives a big Dodge four-by-four. He'll take care of our Lindy. Don't you worry."

Panic attacks. The words echoed long after the older man drove off. Travis stood rooted to the road, watching

Lindy cut through the cemetery, his eyes glued to the mass of bobbing blond curls. He didn't blink until she disappeared over a hill.

Panic attacks. Guilt slammed him with a vicious force. No wonder she hated him. She'd lost so much because of him, but he never would've envisioned Lindy being afraid of cars.

Travis raked his fingers through his hair, still staring in the direction Lindy had disappeared. He could understand her fears. Hell, he'd battled his own nerves the first few times back behind the wheel. And, ironically, he hadn't been injured during the accident. But Lindy had. For the second time in her life she'd survived a fatal car crash, while those she loved had not.

He'd never forget the anguish in her eyes, the pain in her voice, the night she told him about the sleeping trucker who'd crossed a highway center line and crushed her family's station wagon. Lindy had been trapped in the car with her lifeless parents for four hours, waiting for help to arrive.

And then last year, on a rainy night, he and Lindy were arguing—again—as they drove home from a business party he'd dragged her to. A flash of red caught his attention. He swerved to miss the oncoming minivan. His Lexus spun out. The passenger side slammed into a light pole, breaking Lindy's arm, killing their unborn son, destroying their marriage.

He rubbed the ache over his heart as he walked back to his car. Almost a year later, Travis could still see the heartbreak on Lindy's face as she huddled in the front seat of his crumpled car, blood dripping from the gash on her forehead, her arm clamped across her abdomen, her thighs locked tightly together.

He'd failed her. No matter how badly he wanted it, he didn't deserve Lindy's forgiveness. And she didn't deserve all the misery he'd caused in her life.

No matter what it took, he *would* find a way to make up for all that he'd taken from her. He owed her that much. And he always paid his debts.

Chapter Two

When Travis awoke the next day, bright sunshine filled his rented room. He wedged his head off the feather pillow and squinted at the clock: 12:37.

Crap, I'm running late.

After the funeral yesterday, he'd driven aimlessly for hours, making so many laps around Land's Cross he now knew every bump in every road. He'd finally quit trying to outrun his thoughts and returned to the boardinghouse, took a cold shower and flopped into bed. Then stared at the popcorn-textured ceiling until exhaustion dragged him under around dawn.

Forcing himself to sit, elbows propped on his naked thighs, he buried his aching head in his hands. The rural silence rang in his ears, competing with the throbbing beat of his pulse. Fingers pressed against his closed eyelids, he listened to the birds singing outside.

What the devil are they so happy about?

Oh, yeah. They didn't have to face a distrusting wife and a scheming attorney in an hour.

Groaning, he stood and headed for the shower, hoping the Sheltering Arms didn't skimp on the water pressure. Twisting from the waist, he tried to unkink the knots threaded into his spine. He thought longingly of his king-size mattress at home.

His feet stilled as Lindy's words filled his memory. *Being tied to man who'd rather fold himself onto a bed too short and too narrow to be the slightest bit comfortable than share a king-size bed with me.*

That lumpy old guest room bed was the last place on earth he'd wanted to be. He'd ached to lie beside his wife, to comfort her, love her. But he'd been afraid of her reaction, worried she wouldn't want to be anywhere near him. And after the way he'd failed her, he certainly wouldn't have blamed her.

Fighting off the memories, Travis showered and shaved. He had to admit, being named in Lionel Lewis's will had piqued his curiosity. What was the old man up to?

He'd find out soon enough. Gathering his keys and wallet, Travis picked up his cell phone. Amazingly he'd forgotten to turn it back on after the funeral. Probably the first time in years he'd been unreachable for more than an hour.

He switched the phone on. The voice mail icon flashed, indicating a full mailbox. Before he could retrieve his messages, the phone vibrated.

"Monroe."

"Travis, thank God."

Travis heard the anxiety in his brother's voice. He was in trouble. Again. "Who'd you screw with this time, Grant?"

"Whoa, man, don't take my head off. I was beginning to get worried. I must've called you at least a dozen times yesterday, but you never answered." He sounded concerned, but Travis knew better. The only person Grant ever worried about was Grant.

"I turned my phone off."

"Holy crap. She must be a knockout."

"What are you talking about?" Travis paced the small confines of his hotel room, wishing he'd waited another two minutes to turn his phone back on.

"Well, if your phone's off that must mean you've finally put an end to your monklike ways. So, who is she?"

Angry blue eyes flashed through Travis's memory. "God, Grant. Are you ever going to grow up?"

"God, Travis, are you ever going to lighten up?"

Travis wrenched loose the tie he'd just knotted and roughly freed his top button. Everything about his life was constricting these days. "I don't have time to play games. What kind of trouble are you in?"

"Not trouble, exactly."

"What then, *exactly?*"

"Dad fixed me up with the spinster daughter of some business associate. Promised her old man I'd take her to the Spring Fling at the Country Club tonight."

"Which business associate?"

"Burt Tanner."

The leather strap squeezing Travis's brain tightened. Had Winston Monroe lost his mind? A blind date between Grant and their banker's only daughter?

"Grant, what does your social life have to do with me?"

"I need you to take the wallflower. I've got a hot date with your old flame."

Grant hooking up with Julia Wellborne? Could plague and pestilence be far behind?

"Did you make this date before or after you found out about your date with Tanner's daughter?"

"What does that matter?"

"After. That figures, you selfish jerk."

Grant tried to interrupt, but Travis spoke over him.

"You don't have a choice, Grant. If you stand Susan Tanner up, her father's gonna be pissed. Monroe Enterprises needs his financial support to complete the Downtown Renovation Project."

"I don't need a lecture." Petulance filled Grant's voice, proving his words a lie. "I need you take the dog to the party."

"What you need is to learn that your actions have consequences. If you screw this up, you'll blow a ten-million-dollar deal. A loss like that'll devastate Monroe Enterprises, and if the company goes under, not only will you lose your free ride, but our employees will be out of work."

Travis pinched the bridge of his nose. Hundreds of people in danger of losing their livelihoods. He couldn't allow Grant's selfishness to destroy all those innocent lives.

"Spare me the St. Travis crap." Grant's words remained hostile, but the resignation in his tone assured Travis his brother wouldn't stand Susan up. But the poor girl was in for the worst date of her life. If he were in Atlanta, Travis knew he'd probably step in, just to save her the embarrassment.

"For once in your sorry life, just do the right thing." Travis severed the connection. Taking a deep breath, he tried to rein in his temper. He thought about the unsigned resignation letter in his desk. One of these days, he was going to sign the damn thing. Then Grant would have to learn to cover his own ass.

He scraped his free hand through his hair and sighed. *Watch over them, Travis. They're not strong like you.*

Those had been his mother's final words, spoken as her hospital door closed softly behind Winston and Grant Monroe. His father and brother had been too cowardly to stay till the end.

Once he'd promised to take care of the weaker men, his mother's thin hand had squeezed his. Gratitude had filled her eyes. Then she was gone.

Losing his mother, the one person who'd honestly loved him, had left a hole in his heart. For years, he'd tried to fill the emptiness by building Monroe Enterprises into an international conglomerate. Work had occupied his time. But the vacancy in his heart had remained. Until— *Lindy.*

"Damn." Travis consulted the clock: 1:50. Stuffing his cell phone into his breast pocket, he grabbed his room key and rushed to his car, not bothering to turn off the lights before he left.

Grateful that Land's Cross was such a small place, Travis flew south down highway 411. Ten minutes was almost enough time for the trip out to Lindy's farm. In Atlanta, he couldn't escape the parking garage in under ten minutes.

He's late. Lindy seethed, pacing the front porch. Travis barged back into her life, made her wish for things she couldn't have, then didn't have the common courtesy to show up on time.

Angry footsteps carried her to the porch's far corner. Before her, twenty-four hundred acres of month-old cornstalks had begun to poke their way out of the earth. Breathing deeply, she sighed and turned, walking calmly back around the porch that circled three-quarters of her home. She leaned her hip against the railing in the opposite corner and smiled.

Unlike the comfort offered by the cornfields, this view pumped her heart rate up a notch. She'd spent the past year transforming these forty acres, molding them to fit dreams she'd harbored since childhood.

The large two-story red barn stood just as it had since her grandfather built it half a century ago. But she'd built the lean-to on the north side herself. It was the heart of Country Daze Farm. Inside, she'd host dozens of school-children daily, teaching them about the care and feeding of livestock. Her hands-on approach would allow kids to gather eggs, pick cotton from its boll, and for the brave-hearted, a chance to milk a real cow.

Beyond the barn, she'd penned off a petting area. She felt that familiar twinge of excitement as she imagined the schoolchildren lavishing attention on the gentler animals.

A flash of metal caught the corner of her eye. Lindy turned away from her dreams of the future and faced her uncertain present head on. An unfamiliar luxury car rolled down the long driveway. It had to be Travis. No one in Holcombe County would spend that much money on a vehicle unless it harvested crops.

Lindy's spine tensed. Watching the silver sedan park

next to Pops's battered old truck, she felt her anger return. Travis's presence here threatened everything: her dreams, her home, her peace.

He stepped from the car and squinted in her direction, barely giving the farm around him a second glance. *Guess he assessed the property's value during yesterday's visit.*

Clutching her arms across her chest, tucking shaking hands into her folded elbows, she stomped back to the center of the porch, temper mounting with each step.

Arrogant fool. Did he think her grandfather had left him anything of value? He probably already had plans to mow down the crops and build a mall. As if she'd let him get his big-city developer hands on *her* land. No way. She'd rather sell the farm to one of those crazy emu ranchers.

Angry tears gathered behind her eyes. Blinking them back, she spun away from the well-dressed man climbing the front steps and scrambled for the front door.

But she didn't move fast enough. Somehow, Travis got there first, grabbing the knob with one hand and resting the other on her shoulder. He touched her nowhere else, but his warmth penetrated the skin on her back. She felt wrapped up in him.

The uniquely Travis scent of cedar and sea breeze filling her senses also stirred her memory, reminding her of the many times she'd sought comfort in his embrace.

She shrugged away from his touch, but he still held the door closed, imprisoning her within his personal space.

"Lindy, I'm not the enemy."

"You shouldn't be here."

"Well, I am."

"I don't want you to be."

Travis stood so close Lindy felt him flinch as her words hit their target. "Believe me, that's painfully obvious. But until we figure out what your grandfather has done, I'm not going anywhere. Don't make this any harder than it has to be by treating me like the bad guy."

The quiet calm of his voice was hard to resist. It would be so easy to lay her burdens at his feet and allow Travis, a professional problem solver, to make all the hard decisions, deal with the unpleasantness. But taking advantage of Travis's overdeveloped sense of duty would make her no better than his manipulating brother and father.

Nope. No matter what, she wouldn't sacrifice her pride by taking the coward's way out again.

Lifting her chin, she eyed him over her shoulder. "If you want to make this easier, go home. I'm sure you have pressing family business in Atlanta that needs your undivided attention."

Another bull's-eye. This man really brought out her inner bitch.

Lindy held her guilt in check as Travis closed his eyes for an extra long second, drawing air through his teeth. She'd seen him do that a hundred times and knew he fought his temper. When he opened his eyes, she saw he hadn't quite won the battle.

"Like it or not, right now I have pressing family business in Land's Cross that needs my undivided attention." His eyes locked on to hers. Lindy felt sucked into the emotional depths of the swirling green and gold whirlpools. She saw questions there, remembered the warmth she'd often seen reflected in his eyes. The passion. At one time she'd been foolish enough to imagine love shimmering in his eyes.

The echo of tires crunching down the driveway ended their visual standoff. Travis stepped back, leaving her feeling bereft.

Chester, briefcase in hand, climbed out of his truck and approached the porch. The older man wore his poker face. Lindy's already frazzled nerves unfurled further. Intuition assured this meeting wouldn't end well.

Before Chester could ease the tension with social niceties, Lindy pounced. "What's going on, Chester? What have y'all done?"

Chester blew out a frustrated breath and tightened the grip on his briefcase. "First things first. Let's go inside and have a seat. Before we can discuss the specifics, we need to have a formal reading of the will."

Travis finally opened the door and waved his palm, inviting her to precede him inside. Lindy crossed the threshold, feeling as though she'd stepped into a Monet painting. Everything remained recognizable, but nothing was clear.

Walking blindly past the family room, she headed down the hall and veered right, leading the way into Pops's study. Perched on the edge of the seat farthest from the door, she forced herself not to fidget. Once the will was read, she'd know what Pops had done; she'd know exactly what she was up against.

After Travis took his seat, Chester pulled a long manila folder from his briefcase and sat behind the wide oak desk. He slipped reading glasses on his nose, opened the folder and picked up the pages inside. He began to read without preamble.

"I, Lionel Charles Lewis, being of sound mind and body…"

Those words, more than any spoken thus far, brought the truth home to Lindy. Pops was gone. She was alone. Chester's voice droned in her ears, but like Reverend Hollister's eulogy yesterday, Lindy couldn't concentrate on the words.

Never-to-be-repeated scenes filled her memory. Pops tucking a frightened little girl into bed, reminding her that her parents would always be alive in her heart. Pops feeding her cheese grits and wiping away her tears as she struggled through the forgettable woes of puberty. Pops welcoming her home after she'd left Atlanta like a coward, slipping away without a word to her husband.

How would she survive without his strength? His love? Her knees knocked together and her teeth began to chatter.

I'm losing it.

No, she couldn't lose control. She locked her knees and clenched her jaw. Pops would not appreciate a weepy show of emotions. Respect for the man who'd raised her since she'd been orphaned at the age of eight demanded she pack away her tears.

Determinedly, she dragged her attention back to Chester, who was still reading her grandfather's words out loud.

"…a long and happy life. I've done a few things I'm not proud of, and I've thanked God every day of my life for the love of a good woman. Lindy girl, you're a lot like your grandmother. You've got her good heart. I can only hope you turn out to be as understanding and forgiving as my Muriel."

A postmortem apology? Lindy couldn't contain the sob that hiccuped from between her lips.

Her skin tingled as Travis's hand intertwined with hers. She tried to jerk away, but his fingers flexed, holding her hand in place. The strength of his grip offered much-needed reassurance. Her fingers relaxed beneath his. Lindy knew his support was temporary. But for a moment, she didn't feel so alone.

"Lindy girl," Chester's voice continued, but the words were pure Pops, "I've loved you since the night you drew your first breath. All I've ever wanted is your happiness. In the months to come, I hope you can remember that.

"So, to the business at hand. I, Lionel Charles Lewis, leave my entire estate to my granddaughter, Lindy Lewis Monroe, and her husband, Travis Monroe. I make but one stipulation. For a period of no less than one hundred and fifty-four days, they must both reside at the Lewis Family Farm as husband and wife. Should either party refuse, my entire estate shall become a refuge for New Zealand swamp frogs. Neither party shall benefit in any way from this transaction."

No, Pops. That's over. He never wanted me.

Travis's grip became painful, but Lindy welcomed the discomfort, sure that without it, she'd have slid to the floor.

Turning her head to study Travis, she found him staring holes into Chester. She noted the muscle jumping again at his jawline. Angry waves rolled off him.

His anger didn't have anything on hers. For him, this was just a bump in the road. *She* could lose everything.

"How dare he!" Lindy pulled her hand free from Travis's iron grip and jumped to her feet. "How dare you write that fool thing up, Chester. You can't really expect us to honor such drivel."

"Trust me, girl, I did everything I could to talk him out of it, but you know how stubborn he was. I knew if I didn't draft the papers, he'd find someone else who would. Someone less discreet." Chester's mouth folded into a grim frown.

Lindy stalked around the guest chairs, into the open space in the middle of the room. She needed to move before she exploded. One hundred and fifty-four days. She'd lose her mind, cooped up with Travis for that long.

And what the hell were New Zealand swamp frogs?

Lindy paced to the door and back, rubbing her fingertips against her throbbing temples. Her heart pounded against her chest hard enough to bruise the skin.

Travis remained frozen in his chair, narrowed eyes riveted to Chester.

"Why, Chester?" she asked. "Why did he do this? And such an odd time period? What's the significance of one hundred fifty-four days?"

"Lionel felt the two of you gave up too soon. A marriage takes time and work, especially when you hit a rough patch." The old man leaned back in his chair, lacing his fingers over his rounded belly. "One hundred and fifty-four days is how long the two of you lived together as man and wife."

Stunned, Lindy stopped pacing. The muscles in her legs went limp. She slithered into her vacant chair.

She'd been certain one hundred and fifty-four days was forever. But as a measuring stick for her marriage, it sounded pathetically short.

The desk chair squeaked as Chester sat forward. "Lionel figured if he forced you two together, you'd find a way to work things out. He didn't want pride or fear to cause you to wait until it was too late." His voice gentled. "He knew tying up the farm was the only way to get you to make a move, Lindy."

Her grandfather's best friend swiveled his chair, meeting Travis's stare. After silently studying the younger man for several long seconds, Chester spoke, his gentle tone forgotten.

"Lionel spoke highly of you, young man. Felt certain you'd be there for Lindy if her dreams were threatened. I'd say the fact you haven't already stormed out of here proves the old goat got a few things right, even if his method was a little off."

"A little off!" Lindy leaped back to her feet. "He's trying to control our lives. Did he really think we'd just roll over and say, 'Oh, what the heck? The old man's probably got a point. Why don't we just ignore what we want and give this a shot?'"

Travis's hand rested on her shoulder. She hadn't even heard him stand. She didn't shrug off the contact, but she did resist the urge to lean backward. It would be so easy to lose herself in the temporary security of his arms.

"Lindy, calm down." He tenderly squeezed her shoulder. "Your grandfather must've known he wasn't well. What he's done is meddlesome. And insulting. But I think it was his way of looking out for you."

"Why can't anyone see I can take care of myself!" Hands fisted, she itched to pace, but there was nowhere left to go. Dominating men surrounded her.

Travis's other hand grabbed her shoulder, spinning her so quickly she nearly lost her balance. She raised her face to his, shocked to see anger boiling in his eyes.

"That's always been your biggest problem." Travis's voice was low, despite the way his chest heaved. His hands fell from her shoulders and he took a step backward, as if he didn't trust himself not to take a swing at her. She'd never seen this side of Travis.

"Just because you're capable of taking care of everything yourself doesn't mean you've failed if you let someone else handle things sometimes. Or, God forbid, share the burden. You think your fears make you weak." He pivoted with military precision, turning his back on her, stalking to the window.

"Being strong doesn't mean doing it all by yourself," he told her over his shoulder. "Sometimes, it takes more strength to trust someone than it does to go it alone."

Tears burned Lindy's eyes. "When you trust someone and they let you down, it hurts *worse* than going it alone!"

"Yeah, I know." Travis turned and found her eyes. "*You* taught me that lesson."

Travis stared out the study window, searching the clouds for answers, ignoring Chester Warfield's perusal. An awkward, suffocating silence engulfed the room.

What the hell was he supposed to do now? He couldn't let Lindy lose her home, her dreams. On the other hand, he didn't think he could endure one hundred and fifty-four days of living with a woman who so obviously despised him.

Surely he could find a way to fix this. He needed a plan. First step, get his attorney involved. If anyone could find a loophole in the will, it was Brad Middleton. They needed a valid reason to contest the insane terms of the will.

Whoa. Maybe that was it. The terms were unquestionably insane. If they could claim—

"You're thinking too hard, boy," Warfield declared, breaking into Travis's thoughts. "Say what's on your mind."

He turned and faced his wife. "How about having Lionel declared incompetent and ruling the changes invalid?"

"What!" Lindy's cheeks bloomed with angry color.

Warfield ignored her outburst. "If you could convince a judge Lionel wasn't in his right mind, you could probably get the will overturned. Only problem is, there isn't a person in this county, hell, the whole state, that would say Lionel Lewis was anything other than ornery and stubborn. And those aren't grounds for incompetency."

"I can't believe you'd even suggest such a thing!" Lindy's fists balled at her sides. "There's no way I'd do or say anything to ruin my grandfather's good name."

Trying to ignore his wife, Travis turned his concentration to the attorney. He needed all the facts before he took action.

"So, as things stand, in order for Lindy to inherit the farm, I've got to move in with her for a period of one hundred and fifty-four days?"

Warfield nodded. "Correct."

Roughly five months. Long enough to earn her forgiveness? Maybe. Maybe not.

"Do we have to sleep together every night?" he asked.

"Ex-*cuse* me?"

Neither man acknowledged Lindy's outburst, but Travis rephrased his question. "Do we both have to be in residence on the farm every night during that time period? I have a business to run. What if I need to travel?"

Warfield rubbed his chin as though contemplating the question, but Travis noticed the smile he fought to hide. Apparently the old man was beginning to enjoy Travis's dilemma.

"While short business trips are a common component of married life these days, the intention is for the two of you to spend time together. Therefore, you must limit yourself to no more than three nights away per month."

"Darned fool," Lindy grumbled from across the room. Travis wasn't sure exactly which one of them she referred to.

"Does 'husband and wife' imply anything other than living under the same roof? Presenting ourselves as a couple in the community?" Travis wouldn't put anything past Lindy's grandfather at this point. Not even manipulating their sex life.

"No. The wording was chosen to ensure you both reside at the farmhouse without any other live-in guests." The attorney leaned forward in his chair, stacking his forearms on the desk. "I know this is hard for the two of you to believe, but Lionel thought he'd be doing you a favor by arranging this."

"Bull—" Lindy reentered the conversation with a very unladylike comment. "If Pops thought I'd be grateful for this little scheme, he wouldn't have kept it secret. He knew I'd be pissed. He also knew I'd consider it if it was my only way to keep the farm."

"It's not the only way, Lindy," Travis said, but he knew it was. She'd never endorse petitioning for Lionel's incompetency.

"Yes, it is. I won't ruin his reputation. Not for anything in this world. And that includes the farm."

"Final question." Travis readdressed the attorney. "What happens after we serve the hundred fifty-four days?"

Warfield no longer bothered to hide his smile. The old man was definitely getting a kick out of this.

"That's between you and your wife, Mr. Monroe."

Chapter Three

The next morning, Lindy stood before her closet, surveying her wardrobe. Did she really own two dozen pairs of jeans? Yep. And five sets of overalls? Yep, again.

Where were her girl clothes?

Bypassing her extensive denim collection, she dug far in the back of her closet and unearthed the most feminine thing she owned, a periwinkle-blue dress with a full skirt and three-quarter-length sleeves. *Ah, yes. This should do just fine.*

Not bothering with the back zipper, she tugged the dress over her head and smoothed the fabric over her hips until the hem fell to her midcalves. The lightweight jersey knit clung to her curves. And the color certainly set off her eyes.

She fluffed her curls, dabbed on her favorite floral perfume, and pulled out her only tube of lipstick. Pursing her colored lips, she twisted in front of the mirror, surveying herself from every direction. Despite the dark circles under her eyes, she looked ready to handle today's mission.

She'd tossed and turned all night, struggling to find a way out of this mess. Around one in the morning, a crazy idea had popped into her head. By the time she got out of bed this morning at five-thirty, the idea had grown into a full-fledged plan. Now, she just had to find the courage to see it through.

Once she refused to honor the will, she'd be on her own. If she wanted to make a success of Country Daze without involving Travis in her grandfather's crazy scheme, she needed cash.

This morning's trip to the bank was the first step. She refused to let her dreams slip through her fingers again. Making Country Daze a reality had saved her sanity over the past year. She'd lost Travis, their child and now Pops. Her dream was all she had left.

Down on her knees, she rummaged through the boots and dirty sneakers on her closet floor, digging up a comfy pair of sandals. Before she lost her nerve, she slipped them on and dashed downstairs, ducking into the kitchen to grab her keys just as Alice Robertson let herself in the back door.

Her neighbor let out a wolf whistle that would've made any construction worker proud. "Lord Almighty. You look like a girl."

"I sure hope so." Despite the heaviness in her heart, Lindy put her hands on her hips and struck a runway pose. "Girls are the best bait for a manhunt."

Alice raised one red brow. "Gracious, child, no need to set out the bait. You could have any man in Holcombe County with just the wiggle of one finger."

Yeah, right.

"I think I'll stick to my plan." She bussed her lips across Alice's cheek. "Wish me luck."

"Whatever you're up to, that dress oughta be all the luck you need."

Lindy grabbed a sweater off the hall rack and raced outside to Pops's old truck, anxious to get this charade behind her. Her stomach felt like one huge ball of nerves. At three o'clock this morning, she'd been sure her idea was foolproof. Under the bright lights of morning, though, doubts crept in. Pressing her foot against the accelerator, Lindy increased her white-knuckled grip on the steering wheel and did her best to block out her second thoughts.

At precisely nine o'clock, she parked her old truck in the front row of the People's Bank Building. More than ready to escape the close confines of the cab, she snatched her purse off the bench seat and quickly hopped down.

Pretending to rummage through her purse, she stood at the curb for a minute, gulping in fresh air and willing her heart rate to settle. She hated this whole weak-kneed, churning-stomach feeling she got every time she forced herself to drive.

With a final loud exhale, she walked through the double glass doors and entered the bank's lobby. Pinning a confident smile in place, she approached the woman who'd been the bank's receptionist for over twenty years.

"Good morning, Mrs. Carstairs."

"Good morning, Lindy dear. I sure was sorry to hear about Lionel."

Lindy's face curved into the same grateful expression she used every time she heard that sentiment. Pops had been such a popular man, she knew she'd still be accepting condolences a year from now.

"Thank you. How's Lucy doing?"

"She's carrying low. Sure sign the baby's a boy."

Lindy felt a twinge of envy, but pushed it aside. "That's fantastic." She rested one hand on the faux-marble reception desk and flattened the other over her twittering stomach. This was it. No more stalling. Time to do what had to be done.

"Is Mr. Harper in this morning?" No turning back now.

The receptionist's penciled-on eyebrows rose. "Why certainly, dear. Have a seat and I'll let him know you're here."

Resisting the urge to make a break for it and forget the whole thing, she settled into an overstuffed chair. In less than two minutes, Mark Harper appeared from behind a wall of smoky glass. His ever-present pocket protector overflowed with pens and his thick glasses hung precariously on the tip of his nose. He was still too thin for his height and he needed a haircut. And he represented her only chance at escaping this predicament.

Hating herself for what she was about to do, Lindy imposed a fake wobble in her voice and extended her hand to one of the nicest guys she'd ever known. "Mark, thanks for seeing me."

"N-no problem, Lindy. Come on in." He placed his hand on her back and ushered her into his office. His perspiration dampened the material at her waist.

Yep. She was about to do a really despicable thing. But Pops had her cornered.

Fifteen minutes later, Lindy stormed out of the bank building, so angry she didn't know whether to spit or cry.

Unfortunately she could do neither in the middle of the town square.

Focused solely on getting the hell out of Dodge before she lost control of her temper and no longer cared about making a public spectacle of herself, Lindy blindly marched to her truck.

A creative string of curses dripped off her tongue as she dug into her purse for her keys. A familiar whiff of cedar drifting on a sea breeze distracted her. She raised her head, pointed her nose into the wind, and walked straight into the source of the smell.

Travis's hands gripped her elbows to steady her. "Whoa. Are you all right?"

"Yes, I'm all right. Why do people keep asking me that?" Lindy threw back her head and tried to look him in the eye. The sun haloed his head, blocking his face. "Are you following me?"

He laughed, a dry, humorless sound. "No, Lindy. I'm not following you. I just finished breakfast at Daisy's Diner. But I *was* on my way to see you. I checked out of the Sheltering Arms this morning. If we're going to honor the will, we need to make some plans."

Well, she'd already made her plans, and they'd blown up in her face. Dolled up like some backwoods femme fatale, she'd embarrassed both herself and softhearted Mark Harper.

She'd been so sure she could bamboozle him into loaning her enough money to buy the old Roosevelt farm. At just under four hundred acres, it offered less property than her family's farm, but was more than enough land for Country Daze.

But thanks to Pops's wild stipulations, she wouldn't

have any collateral until she fulfilled the terms of the will and inherited her own farm free and clear.

She harrumphed at the fabulous-smelling man in front of her. "I'm sick to death of plans. Plans never work out." She tried to sidestep him, but he refused to release his hold on her elbows. "Let go of me, Travis. I have to get out of here. Right now."

She glared at him through eyes she knew were wet with unshed tears, uncertain how much longer her control would hold.

He leaned forward, bringing his mouthwatering scent with him. Without the sun directly behind his head, his expression became clear. The understanding in his green-gold eyes further threatened her self-control.

"Then let's get out of here." Stepping back, he waved his arm toward her old truck. "Lead the way. I'll follow you."

Tears and emotions back under control, Lindy drove under the Lewis Family Farm archway, one eye glued to the BMW tailing her. *Now what?*

Her brilliant plan to outsmart Pops had failed. That left her with only two options. Walk away from her home and her dreams or bury her pride and ask for Travis's help.

"Talk about your rock and a hard place." She turned off her old truck and sat for a moment, fiddling with the keys, delaying the inevitable. For the first time in over a year, she didn't feel the overwhelming urge to escape the vehicle.

Stunned to realize worrying about Travis had blocked out her normal nervousness during the entire drive home, she climbed slowly from the cab. As her feet hit solid ground, a breeze caught her hem, whipping the dress around her knees.

Travis rolled to a stop. Pretending to ignore him while she smoothed her skirt back into place, she watched from under her lashes as he stepped from the car, first one expensive Italian leather shoe, then the next. Straightening, he shut the door and engaged his car alarm.

A sardonic grin twisted her lips. Was he afraid the chickens might try to make off with his fancy car?

He's so out of place here. The hard truth sobered her, flattening her grin into a frown.

All those months she'd spent dreaming of Travis coming for her, putting their marriage before his family's selfish demands, she'd never once considered what would happen after his arrival. Seeing him here, standing in the barnyard wearing a coat and tie, she realized this man would never fit into her life.

Raising her head, she caught him openly studying her. His eyebrows rose, waiting for her to make the next move. She strode onto the porch. His footsteps followed. She opened the front door, but paused on the threshold, once again meeting his gaze over her shoulder.

"You don't fit in here." A simple statement of fact, but saying it aloud brought an unexpected lump to her throat.

"I'm willing to try," Travis said, following her inside.

"I'm not sure I am." She slammed the heavy front door, automatically toeing out of her shoes, even though the sandals she'd worn to town were free from barnyard yuck.

Travis gripped her arm, spun her around. Even in the unlit entryway, she could see the angry pulse jumping at his temple. His eyes narrowed and he opened his mouth.

What he would've said, she'd never know.

"Lindy!" Shayna Miller, her assistant, neighbor and childhood friend, called out from the kitchen. "I thought you'd never get home!"

Fast footfalls echoed down the hallway. Travis growled low in his throat and dropped her arm, but didn't move. Lindy did, stepping outside his aura of controlled energy, reestablishing her personal space.

"They're here!" The petite brunette rounded the corner at full speed and skidded to a stop, barely missing a direct collision with Travis. "Wow, he *is* gorgeous." Her soft brown eyes rolled in embarrassment. "Oh, gosh. I'm sorry."

Lindy snuck a peek at her handsome husband. "Yeah, me, too."

Travis extended his hand, gracefully ignoring Shayna's faux pas. "Good morning. I'm Travis."

Poor Shayna. At twenty-four, only two years younger than Lindy, she was totally unprepared for Travis's well-honed charm. Or his sexy smile.

"Shayna Miller," she gushed. Her blush deepened as she tentatively grasped his large hand.

"Nice to meet you, Shayna. Sounds like you've got big news."

Amazing. She'd forgotten how easily he could avert social disaster with a smile and a handshake. She'd seen him do it hundreds of times on the cocktail-party circuit.

"Oh, yeah." Embarrassment forgotten, Shayna turned to Lindy. "They finally came. The delivery van brought 'em this morning. Rufus barked like crazy."

"Shayna?" Lindy asked when her friend paused for a breath.

"Yes?"

"What came?"

Shayna giggled. "Sorry. I'm just so exci—"

"Shayna!"

"The picnic tables and benches. Ooh, they're so tiny and cute. It all looks pretty ratty now, but once we repaint them they'll be so precious."

Lindy plopped into one of the wing chairs just inside the family room. The picnic tables. Ten of them. And *twenty* benches. The prepaid, nonrefundable picnic tables and benches she'd bought at an online auction.

Ten picnic tables weren't enough to accommodate her long-range plans for Country Daze, but her budget insisted she make do her first couple of years. This purchase had stretched her already burdened credit card to its limit.

Her mind spun with details. After so many years of hoping and planning, her dream was within her grasp. If she lost the farm, she'd lose everything.

"Lindy, what's wrong?" Shayna stooped in front of her, worry lines etched between her eyes. "You've lost all your color. Are you sick?"

"No, I'm not sick. I'm stuck." She rubbed her palm over her forehead, scraping her hair back. Tilting her head, resting her chin in her palm, she stared at Travis. He stood there, staring back, looking strong and reliable. But could she trust him?

I don't have a choice.

"Shayna, why don't you go on home for today? Travis and I have some things to settle." She gave her friend a weak smile.

"Are you sure?"

"Yes. I'm sure." The conviction in her voice pleased Lindy. At least she sounded like a woman in control.

Travis still leaned against the door frame. Lindy felt the pressure of his eyes, like a finger lifting her chin, demanding her full attention.

She met his gaze, calling on every ounce of her Lewis pride to hold his stare. Emerald and gold swirled together, offering understanding, threatening to break the seal on emotions she'd packed away months ago.

How would she get through this without sacrificing her pride? Or her heart?

Their gazes remained locked, their lips still, as Shayna gathered her things and let herself out. Neither moved until the back door snicked closed. Finally Travis straightened from his doorway slouch. "Should I sit?"

She noted the lack of humor in his voice, relieved to know he took this situation as seriously as she did.

Lindy lurched to her feet, bumping the upholstered chair against the wall. She was about to admit defeat, accept the terms of the will, invite Travis into her home.

She needed a moment alone before she surrendered.

"Make a pot of coffee first," she ordered. "I'll be right back."

Travis stared out the window over the kitchen sink, studying the tiny green sprigs dotting the fields of dark soil. What did she grow here? Did she make a profit? Was she happy? There was so much he didn't know about farm life. So much he didn't know about his wife.

Behind him, the coffeepot chimed. Grateful for the activity, he pulled down two mugs and turned to the fridge for Lindy's cream. Two cow-shaped magnets secured an August calendar page to the freezer door. An orange smiley face marked the second Monday with the words Opening Day written underneath. Each weekday block for the rest of the month contained the name of a least one school followed by the number of children in their group.

Intrigued, he lifted a bottom corner and found the page for September. Almost every school day was already booked.

A soft shuffling noise alerted him to her presence. "Looks like you're going to be very busy this fall," he commented without turning around.

"You should see the spring schedule." She sounded tired, sad.

He doctored both their coffees before turning to face her. She *looked* tired. Sad. Travis wanted to hold her. Instead he carried the two mugs to the table, set them on opposite ends and took his seat.

Lindy laid the yellow legal pad and pen she carried next to her cup. Pulling out the chair, she folded her right leg into the seat and sat.

He could see the decision in her eyes. She was going to accept the terms of the will, but she wouldn't meekly lie down and let life steamroll her. He'd bet his last nickel she still had a lot of fight left in her.

"Before we go any further," she said, "I want to know why you're willing to do this."

Dangerous question.

He took a sip of his sugared coffee, and for half a second considered telling her the whole truth. How would she react if she knew about the many nights he woke, covered in sweat, haunted by the look of devastation on her face the night their son died? What if he told her part of him died that night, too, that he'd do anything to make up for the pain and loss he'd caused her? What if, God forbid, he admitted what a wasteland his life had become since the day she left?

She'd spit in his face, that's what. Lindy obviously didn't want him in her life. No sense putting himself out there just so she could trample him again on her way out the door.

Best stick with a partial truth. "Because, after everything that's happened, I don't want to see you suffer anymore."

Her eyes narrowed, as if she waited for the other shoe to drop, certain it couldn't be as simple as that.

"I also have a selfish reason." Oh, he loved the way she raised that chin, telling him loud and clear she thought he was full of bull.

"I've been trying to distance myself from Monroe Enterprises. A couple months of AWOL should do the trick."

Lindy's brows knotted. Travis could almost see the questions forming in her head.

"You expect me to believe you plan to go five months without working?"

"I don't intend to stop working." He ran a frustrated hand through his hair. This was the first time he'd discussed his plans with anyone other than his attorney and best friend, Brad Middleton.

"There's a huge potential in renovating old buildings and turning them into condos. The revitalization of metropolitan downtown districts is becoming big business. The board of directors doesn't agree, so I've decided to branch off and start my own company." He shrugged. The skeptical look on Lindy's face made him glad he'd opted against explaining his more personal motives.

"Get real, Travis. No one knows better than I do how much the family business controls you. You'd never just walk away."

"My goals are different these days." During their marriage, he'd worked extra hard, putting in long hours, building a legacy to leave his child. Now that he didn't have a son, he no longer needed a legacy. "I'm not quitting Monroe Enterprises altogether. Not yet, at least. With my laptop, Internet access and a fax machine, I can keep an eye on things from here."

He paused, taking another sip of coffee. "Besides, I owe your grandfather one."

"What's that supposed to mean?"

"I promised him I'd take care of you and our baby. I failed."

"Losing the baby wasn't your fault." Her voice hitched, but she kept her chin level with his.

"If I'd been paying attention to the road, that van never would've hit us."

Lindy's blue eyes suddenly sparkled with tears. She sniffed into her coffee cup, obviously fighting for control. Travis's gut tightened. He'd give anything to go back in time, to avoid that drunk driver, to be able to keep Lindy and their son safe.

He watched as Lindy studied the elaborate doodle she created on the legal pad. She sat without talking so long, Travis wondered if the conversation was over.

Then she flipped the doodle page over and looked up, a very determined gleam in her eyes. "If we're going to do this, I have some ground rules." She wrote Ground Rules across the top of the page and underlined it three times.

Uh-oh. That didn't sound good. Did she plan on making him sleep in the barn? One look at her stubborn Lewis chin convinced Travis such ideas were not improbable.

"Number one." She wrote the number, then dotted the pad firmly. "This is a working farm. We keep farmer's hours, so no loud noises after nine o'clock. Lights out at ten."

Travis nodded, though he sensed her "ground rules" weren't up for debate.

"Number two. The upstairs bedrooms share a common bathroom, so keep it neat. And don't forget to use the lock. Alice Robertson comes in two mornings a week and helps with the housework, but you and I will have to trade off kitchen duty."

"Robertson?" Please God, let her be Farmboy's wife.

"Danny's mother."

Damn!

"Three," Lindy continued. "Without Pops, I'm short-handed. I expect you to help out around here. Danny is familiar with farm work, but he has his own responsibilities and can't be here full-time, so we'll figure out what chores you can handle. The work's hard and dirty, but you're strong enough."

The words sounded complimentary, but he knew better.

"Number four. I will not take any money from you. Don't insult me by trying to cover my expenses behind my back. Things are tight around here. That's how I want it to stay."

Lindy's chin lifted; glittery defiance shot from her eyes.

"Five. No physical contact. This setup is for appearances' sake only." She put the pen on top of the tablet and crossed her arms on the table. He noted the slight tremor in her fingers before she clenched them into fists.

"Do we have a deal?" she asked.

Travis saw through her bravado. He wanted to round the table and sweep her into his arms, hold her until she melted against him, asked for his help, accepted his support. But this was Lindy. Things were never simple with Lindy.

He picked up her discarded pen and turned the tablet around. "I have a couple of conditions of my own." He wrote a bold number six on the first empty line.

Her eyebrow cocked. "Such as?"

"No extramarital dating."

Her forehead crinkled, but she shrugged and nodded. "Okay."

She jumped on that faster than Travis expected. Did she have Farmboy wrapped that tightly around her little finger?

"You're sure Robertson won't object?"

"Why would he? Danny knows how important getting this place up and running is to me. He's willing to help any way he can."

Travis bit back a snort. If Lindy believed her own explanation, she was delusional. And Robertson was a bigger fool than Travis had originally thought.

Putting Robertson aside, Travis added number seven to the list. He cleared his mind, focused on his objective. Lindy had to agree with his final condition. She'd already paid too great a price for his mistakes.

Nothing would ever make things right between them, but her panic attacks were his fault. He had to find a way to alleviate her anxiety.

"Number seven, you let me help you face your fear of cars."

Her face paled. "What? Why?"

"I had my own problems getting back behind the wheel. I understand some of what scares you."

"I don't know…."

"I wasn't afraid to accept any of your conditions."

Lindy's chin popped up. He knew that would get to her.

"All I have to do is try?"

"Just try." Travis fought to hide his growing smile. Pride had always been her Achilles' heel.

"O-okay. I promise to try."

"Then I guess we have a deal." Travis held his hand out.

Lindy stood and clasped it. Her grip was steady, but her palm was moist. "Yes, God help me, we have a deal."

Chapter Four

Travis slowly approached his father's house, dread filling him at the thought of the conversation awaiting him. Reaching the end of the road, he killed the ignition and stared at the house. Throw in a couple of ramparts topped with family-crested flags and the place would look like a bona fide castle.

His father had purchased this monstrosity the year after Carrie Monroe's death, and to Travis, it represented the antithesis of the warm home his mother had created. Despite marrying into one of the richest families in Georgia, she never forgot her roots.

His mother had grown up watching her parents work long hours turning an old family recipe into a profitable chain of restaurants. She'd tried her best to instill those values into her children. She'd succeeded with Travis, but

Grant was too much their father's son to understand the appeal of earning your blessings. Like Winston, Grant considered changing the blade in his razor too tactile a chore for a Monroe.

After his mother's death, living in his father's new house had made Travis feel like a teenage hypocrite. He hated the way Winston immersed himself back into the world of Atlanta's spoiled rich, abandoning his late wife's ideals.

At eighteen, Travis escaped to college, moving to Boston to study mechanical engineering at MIT. After one semester, he returned to this mausoleum and found his father in a near-constant drunken stupor and his fifteen-year-old brother in juvenile lockup. Travis was forced to abandon MIT and transfer to Georgia Tech. He bailed out his brother and dried out his father. Ten years later, very little had changed.

He rolled his shoulders, trying to relieve his building tension. Telling his father about his extended stay in Tennessee promised to be a long conversation. And he still had the six-hour drive back to Land's Cross.

She'll have my butt if I miss curfew on my first night.

He slowly climbed from the car and approached his father's home. The well-worn work boots he'd pulled on this morning echoed like thunder as he crossed the bridge spanning a long, narrow koi pond—Lord Winston's version of a moat.

A corner of his mouth curved upward at his private joke as he rang the bell and waited. Brighton, his father's butler, opened the ten-foot-tall front door. The old man's stoic expression didn't falter as he eyed Travis across the threshold.

"Afternoon, Brighton. Is my father home?"

The butler nodded wordlessly and stepped back, allowing Travis to enter. His bony fingers pushed the massive door closed, blocking out the only natural light in the darkened foyer. "Wait here," the brusque voice ordered. "I'll see if he is available."

Travis watched the man's thin back disappear down the darkened hallway. All the curtains were drawn against the bright afternoon sun. The low-wattage bulbs his father favored didn't stand a chance against the dreary darkness. Directional lighting highlighted several expensive pieces of art throughout the marbled foyer. Despite the rich paintings, the room lacked life.

Unlike Lindy's home, where bright sunlight flooded the entry hall. The windows across the front of the farmhouse were all curtainless. The outside scenery provided more beauty and decoration than a hundred priceless masterpieces.

Travis traced the outline of a painted magnolia bloom with his fingertip. Where this place smelled of musty age and old money, the natural fragrance of flowers and sunshine filled every corner of Lindy's home. And Lindy's kitchen always smelled like cinnamon.

Brighton returned to the foyer, announcing his presence with a chastising clearing of his throat. The man had the eerie ability to show up suddenly in a room; no noise ever preceded him. "Your father will see you now."

As expected, Brighton led Travis into the study, a room that summed up Winston Monroe perfectly. Stuffy, old-fashioned and ostentatious.

"Dad." Travis nodded at the man seated behind the wide mahogany desk and crossed the paneled room, heading directly for the leather-wrapped bar in the far corner.

With his dark hair and green eyes, Travis was the only member of the Monroe clan who carried the family's black Irish coloring into this generation. He bore no resemblance to his father. Their physical differences were almost as startling as their polar opposite lifestyles.

His father had passed a near carbon copy of his genes to Grant—lithe build, light brown hair, hazel eyes, aquiline nose. Country-club handsome, Lindy called them.

"Glad to see you found your way back to town," Winston snapped. "Unlike you to disappear without a word to anybody."

"Marge knew where I was."

Winston snorted. "That damn secretary of yours locks up tighter than Fort Knox."

The image of Winston trying to wheedle information out of Marge brought a small smile to his lips. "I asked her not to reveal my whereabouts unless there was an emergency."

His father's only answer was a "Humph!" Winston Monroe believed everyone had their price. And if his father were this bent out of shape over three days' absence…

Travis considered tipping the bottle over the glass again, knowing this was going to be a two-finger conversation. But he had a long drive ahead of him, so he recapped the decanter and pushed it aside.

He swallowed a sip of the amber liquid, enjoying the sting as Kentucky's finest warmed his throat. "I came by to bring you up to speed on some changes I've put in place at the company."

His father's brows merged into a bushy line of appre-hension. "What kind of changes?"

"I've promoted George Collins to second vice president

and transferred most of my daily responsibilities to him, everything but the final details on the Downtown Renovation Project. Marge will be working with him, so the transition should be smooth."

"Transition? What in blue blazes are you talking about?"

"I'm taking a leave of absence for the summer."

"You can't do that!" Noxious smoke curled from the cigar stub clinging to his father's lower lip.

"It's already done."

Winston squinted. "What are your plans?"

"I'll be working in Tennessee, helping Lindy get a new project off the ground."

His father's fingers shook as he plucked the cigar from his mouth and smashed the butt into an ashtray. "Damn it, boy!" Winston rose from his large, thronelike chair and prowled toward the bar. "Can't you see that girl's using you? First she forces you to marry her—"

"Choose your words carefully, Dad." Travis clenched his fists around his glass, silently reminding himself his mother had once loved this son of a bitch.

His father shot a look across the room, focusing on a painting of Carrie Monroe hanging above the fireplace. He closed his eyes for a long moment, drew in a deep breath. When his lids lifted again, Travis saw icy control in his father's eyes.

"All I'm saying is think about what you're doing. If your *wife* were really interested in you, she'd have stood by you instead of taking off for almost a year. You and I both know what she's after."

Why did his father insist on repeating this same old

argument? "If she'd been after my money, she wouldn't have insisted on a prenup."

The night Lindy told him she was pregnant, he'd proposed immediately. She'd argued that a part-time waitress and college student from nowhere, Tennessee, couldn't marry the heir to Monroe Enterprises. He'd been ready to resign on the spot, but she'd cut him off, saying that for their child's sake, she'd marry him, but not until they'd signed a prenuptial agreement.

Travis swallowed another long sip of his bourbon. "Lindy has never made any claims against the precious Monroe fortune."

"I still say she has a hidden agenda." Just like everyone else in Atlanta, Winston refused to believe Lindy wasn't after his money. They found it unfathomable that someone wanted Travis for himself, not his money or his power or his connections.

"Forget about Cross Landing. Stay here. Let me fix you up with Senator Brown's daughter, Emily. She's an attractive woman with the right kind of background to be a Monroe wife."

"It's Land's Cross, and I won't forget about it. If Emily Brown is such a catch, fix her up with Grant. He needs a new babysitter. I'm getting tired of the job." Travis gulped the last of the bourbon and slammed his glass against the rich maple bar. "Besides, I'm still a married man."

"Don't remind me."

"You'd do well to remember, Dad."

Tense silence filled the room, swelling the air. Travis expected the curtained windows to burst from the pressure.

Discussing Lindy with his father had always been a

waste of time. He just wanted to deal with the business details and get on the road. Lindy was waiting.

"Like it or not, I'm spending the summer in Tennessee with my wife. I'm taking a computer and fax with me and of course my cell phone, so I'll be in constant contact."

His father's eyes narrowed, his face mirroring the spiteful look Grant so often wore when things didn't go his way.

Travis's Irish anger rose. He'd spent his entire adult life trying to single-handedly keep what was left of his family on the right track. No more. There had to be a way for him to keep his word to his mother, safeguard the welfare of his employees and reclaim his life.

Thanks to Lionel Lewis, he had roughly a hundred and fifty days to find the answer.

Lindy sneered at the postcard-perfect sunset framed by her bedroom window. Below the horizon, the half-mile gravel driveway stretched to the highway, undisturbed by travelers.

Where was he?

Darkness was falling, yet lights out was still several hours away. But he promised to be back tonight so that his trip to Atlanta would only count as one night away from the farm.

What if he doesn't show?

That question had rattled around in her head for the past two days, driving her to the brink of insanity. She'd pinned her hopes on Travis again. What if he got back to Atlanta and decided to stay with his family instead of helping her? After all, she'd made it very clear she didn't want him here. Only a true glutton for punishment would return for more of the same.

She'd been a complete bitch since the moment he'd arrived. But damn it, he'd waltzed onto her territory unannounced, threatening her mental well-being and her future. Still, he had agreed to fulfill the outrageous terms of Pops's will. She knew he felt guilty about the loss of their son. A man like Travis would not easily forgive himself for such a thing.

The stuff about branching off from Monroe Enterprises and starting his own company was surely just a cover story. A fabrication he made up to assuage the guilt and embarrassment she felt over Pops's ultimatum. She couldn't imagine Travis walking away from the duty he felt to Winston and Grant.

Whatever his reasons, she would owe him big-time for making such a huge sacrifice. She wanted this farm. She wanted to make Country Daze a reality. She wanted her quiet, uncomplicated life back.

Looking out over the still barnyard, she sighed. As long as Travis remained underfoot, her life would be anything *but* quiet and uncomplicated.

Shoot, after less than a week, he already had her gazing out her window like some overanxious Southern belle expecting her hero to gallop down the walk and rescue her. At this rate, she'd never make it till summer's end without begging for whatever scraps of time and attention Travis threw her way.

Been there. Done that.

During the one hundred and fifty-four days—and nights—of her marriage, Travis had turned her life into a waiting game.

Waiting for Travis to love her. Waiting all day for Travis to call, just to find he'd be home too late for dinner. Waiting until Travis finally came home, then discovering all he wanted was her body.

For Travis, marriage had been a sexual convenience. No more candlelit dinners. No more heartfelt conversations. The only time Mr. and Mrs. Travis Monroe spent together was in bed. And God, what fabulous times those were, but she'd needed more than just sex. Much more.

Once upon a time, she'd dreamed of a true marriage, making a home and family with Travis. She'd foolishly believed love could overcome the differences in their backgrounds, the heartache of losing their child. Had believed it right up to the moment she'd overheard his ex-fiancée, Julia Wellborne, recommend he send "wifey back to the sticks."

Standing outside her husband's office at nine o'clock one night, romantic picnic in her hand and seduction on her mind, she'd waited for Travis to scoff at the woman's suggestion. Instead he'd asked that vile woman how it would look to society if he shipped his wife off so soon after "her unfortunate accident."

The pain of his betrayal had punched so hard, she'd fled to the ladies' room and gotten violently ill. Fool that she was, she'd never realized what an obligation she'd become for Travis. Nor did she realize he was still involved with another woman.

That night, she'd packed a single suitcase, bought a bus ticket and left Atlanta with nothing more than a note to explain her departure. "Travis, I'm going home. Where I belong." Her hand had been shaking so badly, she couldn't even sign her name. Huddled in a cracked vinyl bus seat, she'd cried all the way home, back to Pops, back to the farm.

Now Travis was here, not by choice but, once again, tied to her by obligation.

Despite the heartache and betrayal that had technically, if not legally, ended their marriage, her body still reacted explosively to Travis. Even standing in a cemetery, surrounded by mournful people, he'd made her yearn for things she knew she couldn't have again.

The close confines of the next few months would test her willpower. It was a test she wasn't sure she could pass. Cohabitation, even the forced variety, would more than likely lead them down the same path. She'd end up in his bed. Loving it. Hating it.

Until something or someone more important called him away.

She couldn't let that happen. Adjusting to a Travis-free life a second time would destroy her, because this time she'd be unable to find peace in the land since she'd be indebted to Travis for every square inch.

Hot tears pricked her eyelids. She clenched her lower lip between her teeth. *Do not cry.*

Turning her back on the crimson-hued fields and the vacant driveway, Lindy stalked off to the bathroom, where she could hide her tears in the shower's spray.

Travis pulled to a stop in front of Lindy's home. A little before nine and the place looked deserted, unwelcoming. A motion-sensing lamp over the barn's double doors provided the only light.

Travis silently apologized to his garage-spoiled car as he parked her under the night sky next to Lindy's rusty old truck. He retrieved a single suitcase from the trunk. A large box of files, his laptop and a combo copier and fax occupied the backseat. His portable office setup would have to wait till morning. Right now, all he wanted was a quick bite, a hot shower and some sleep.

The thumbnail moon offered little guidance as he crossed the graveled lot and approached the front porch. The motion-sensing light timed out. Blackness pressed in upon the yard, like the world had suddenly been wrapped tight in a thick wool blanket. His toe missed the second step to the porch, throwing him off balance. The corner of his suitcase banged into the porch rail, ricocheting into his thigh.

For Pete's sake, she knew he'd be back tonight. Would it have killed her to leave a light on? Feeling his way in the darkness, he found the brass knob and turned. The cool metal didn't budge. The house was locked up tight.

Now she locks the door. He refused to stand on the porch and scream for her attention like a Marlon Brando wannabe.

Travis tightened the grip on his black leather bag and stumbled his way around back in the full darkness of a country night. The moonlight shone a bit brighter on the service porch. Travis opened the screen door and eyed the kitchen door. *If this one's locked, too, I'm going to knock it off its hinges. And I won't apologize tomorrow.*

Thankfully he found the door unlocked. The stove lamp was the only light in the house. It provided enough illumination to read the note she'd left him. *Travis, don't forget to lock the door. Chores start at 6:00. a.m.*

She'd underlined the *A* and *M* seven fricking times. Did she think he was a complete imbecile?

The note was unsigned.

Not that he'd expected "Love Lindy" or "Your adoring

wife" scrawled across the bottom of the page. Still, an initial or a quick signature would've been a nice touch. But of course, Lindy specialized in short, unsigned notes that ripped his heart out.

Don't go there, man.

He scrounged up cheese and crackers and a beer for dinner. A cat clock hung on the kitchen wall. Its tail flicked and a soft meow announced the half hour. Thirty minutes till lights out.

Grabbing his suitcase, Travis climbed the stairs, headed for a shower. After dropping off his bag, he unpacked a clean pair of briefs and his shaving kit, stripped off his travel clothes and streaked to the bathroom. And stopped dead in his tracks.

Her unmentionables hung from the shower rod. Nothing fancy, just two flesh-colored bras with lace trim and matching panties. His body responded immediately. He pulled down one bra, caressing its softness across his cheek. It smelled clean and fresh, like Lindy.

"Ah, sweetheart, you're killing me." He removed the other garments and threw them all over his shoulder, not bothering to check where the scraps of silk landed. He dropped his clean underwear and kit next to the sink and flicked the cold water knob on full blast.

Thrusting his head under the icy shower, he tried to convince his body to calm down. But it was no use. All his vital organs—heart, brain, groin—knew Lindy slept in her bed, just the other side of the bathroom wall.

When his alarm sounded at five-thirty, Travis had just drifted off. He didn't bother to open his eyes as he slammed a fist atop the clock radio beside his bed. He stumbled out of bed, desperate to empty his bladder. Some foggy corner of his brain reminded him of his current shared bathroom arrangement, keeping him from charging into the hallway butt-naked.

He tugged on his jeans, not wasting time with the button or zipper, and staggered, squinty-eyed, down the hall and into the bathroom. Once he'd taken care of business, he turned to the sink, leaning his forearms against the smooth ceramic tile, trying to avoid his reflection while dousing his face with cold water.

His fingers probed his stubbled chin, and he contemplated shaving but quickly decided against it. He couldn't have gotten more than two hours' sleep last night, and without the benefit of coffee, shaving would be hazardous to his health.

He smacked his lips, stirring up morning mouth. Brushing his teeth he could handle without caffeine. His shaving kit still sat next to the sink where he'd left it last night. He unzipped it and dug around, finding a toothbrush but no toothpaste.

"Hope you don't mind sharing, roomie," he muttered as he slid out the vanity drawer. "Jackpot." He grabbed for the tube of Crest, but his fingers snagged something stored just behind the toothpaste and pulled the unexpected item out, as well.

All remnants of sleep vanished as he stared at the round dial of pills labeled May. His knees went weak. Lindy was on the Pill? The cardboard packet seemed to burn his fingers. He dropped the pills and slammed the drawer shut.

Early in their relationship, Lindy had told him she didn't like the idea of taking artificial hormones. They'd relied on condoms for birth control. Obviously not a foolproof plan.

Guess she didn't want to risk another accident. With Robertson?

Travis's heart stopped beating. His knees gave out altogether, causing him to stagger backward into the opposite wall. Bile rose in his throat at the image of Lindy with Robertson.

From the hallway, the alarm started buzzing again. Swallowing the hurt and jealousy, he stumbled back to his bedroom. The clock continued to blare, the numbers flashing in neon-green, the same shade as the tiny pills his wife now used to avoid a second unwanted pregnancy.

"Nooooo!" Desperate to vent, he slammed his fist onto the clock. The blow popped the faceplate off and sent the black box scurrying backward. It slipped between the table and the wall, clattering its way to the ground.

Chest heaving, eyes closed, Travis stood next to the bed and focused on slowing his heart rate, evening out his breathing, regaining his control.

Gradually another sound drifted into the room. Not annoying like the alarm clock, but attention-grabbing nonetheless.

"Cock-a-doodle-dooooo!" The rooster's crow penetrated his haze, piercing his anger. Rational thoughts began to trickle in.

Lindy. Barnyard. At 6:00 a.m. Underlined seven fricking times.

I can't be late.

He slowly opened his eyes and looked toward the bedside table to check the time. No clock. "Of course not, you big idiot."

He couldn't remember the last time he'd completely lost

control like that. He'd perfected keeping his temper under wraps those first few months after his mother died.

"God, Monroe, you're losing it." A quick check of his watch showed he had only seven minutes to pull himself together and report for duty. He spent the first two drawing in deep breaths, willing his temper back into its iron box of willpower.

Once he felt somewhat in control, he fastened his jeans and threaded his belt through the loops. The rooster's crow sounded again. He clipped his cell phone to his belt, layered on a couple of shirts, and pulled on his old work boots.

Still needing to brush his teeth, he detoured into the bathroom. Thankfully the toothpaste had landed on the floor so he didn't have to open that godforsaken drawer again. After the worst brushing in dental history, he slapped the light off with undue force and raced downstairs.

By the time he got to the kitchen, the coffeepot was already half empty. He grabbed a cup and a banana and was crossing the barnyard by 5:59.

Lindy was already there. And, surprise, surprise, Farmboy was cozied up to her. Seeing them together, standing so close not even the early morning light could shine between them, threatened Travis's newly regained command of his temper.

Despite the crisp temperature, he felt an angry flush spread across his cheeks. He enjoyed the vision of his fingers wrapped tightly around Farmboy's throat as he advanced on the couple in front of him.

Still a good three steps away, he caught Robertson's eye. Farmboy twined an arm around Lindy and curled his lips back, baring his teeth in what Travis assumed was a smile.

"Morning, Trav. Lindy and I were trying to figure out what chores you might be able to handle without killing the stock. Or yourself." Robertson covered the insult with a chuckle.

He gritted his teeth, knowing full well Farmboy was staking his claim. Travis took a swig of lukewarm coffee and tried to gain control of his emotions.

"I'm sure I'll be too busy to kill anything. Or anyone." Travis vowed not to utter a single complaint, no matter what Robertson came up with. He'd be damned if he'd let the other man know he was the least bit concerned about Robertson's relationship with Lindy.

"Busy's an understatement around here." Lindy stepped away from Robertson. "We don't have time to waste going behind you, Travis, so if you don't understand something, ask." The morning temperature had nothing on the cold stare Lindy threw him.

Travis's male pride noticed Lindy's eyes straying to his mouth, lingering there half a second too long. The pink tip of her tongue flicked over her lips. She quickly lifted her eyes back to his, her cheeks pinker than before.

He shoved the last bite of banana into his mouth, swallowing a groan along with his breakfast.

From inside the barn, a distressed moan broke into the morning's quiet. A small smile played with the edges of Lindy's mouth as she glanced at the barn behind her.

"Well, sounds like the girls are hungry." She and Robertson shared a chuckle.

"What girls?" Travis asked.

"Thelma and Louise. Danny'll introduce y'all." Lindy turned, her fingers trailing across Farmboy's broad right shoulder. "Remember, Dan, he's a city boy. Break him in easy," she said as she walked off, fading into the barn's black interior.

Travis had no idea how long he and Robertson stood eyeing each other in the barnyard. By the time the other man spoke, Travis's coffee mug had become cold against his fingers.

"So help me, if you hurt her again, I'll send you back to the city in a full body cast," Robertson said, puffing out his chest, appearing even more imposing.

Wow. That's one hell of an opening line.

Travis tossed the last cold sip of coffee down his throat like it was the first shot of whiskey after a long, hard day.

"I'm not here to hurt her. I'm here to win her back." He raised his chin to a stubborn level Lindy would've been proud of. "So you'd best keep your hands off my wife."

Chapter Five

My wife. The words sent a possessive rush of heat through Travis's blood, filling him with an archaic need to mark his territory, no matter how unfamiliar the ground might be.

Fire flashed from Robertson's eyes as he widened his stance, flexed his shoulders and shifted his weight to the balls of his feet, like a boxer responding to the first bell.

Travis stepped forward, narrowing the gap. Surprise flickered through Robertson's brown eyes. Most people probably retreated when the giant bowed up, but Travis wasn't most men.

"I'm here for the long haul, Farmboy."

"Long haul, my ass. This life's too hard for soft city boys. You won't last a month."

"Don't bet on it. I gave Lindy my word. I'm not going anywhere until things between us are settled."

"She's supposed to trust your word? All your word's ever brought her is heartache."

"What is it that really bothers you? The idea that I broke her heart? Or the fact that she married me and not you?"

"You sorry sack of manure. No wonder she left you. You've got no respect for marriage. Or Lindy."

It took every ounce of willpower to uncurl his fingers rather than slam his fists into Farmboy's midsection. "My respect for Lindy's the only thing keeping me from knocking you on your ass."

"Little fella like you?" Robertson crossed his arms over his massive chest. "No way."

"Knock it off, guys," Lindy's agitated voice hurtled at them as she emerged from the barn, a pail of eggs in her hand. "Quit strutting and get to work."

Even from across the barnyard, Travis felt her frustration. Reluctantly, he stepped back and forced his shoulders to relax. He'd agreed to her terms, accepted his role as general laborer. Allowing Robertson to bait him wouldn't get the job done.

"Sure thing, babe." Robertson pasted on a stiff smile. "Just wanted to make sure you were through in the barn before I got Trav started mucking out the stalls."

The big man pivoted and walked toward the barn. Travis closed his eyes for a moment, drawing the crisp morning air into his lungs. Mucking the stalls? Oh, man, this was not good. Robertson was bound to make the job even worse than it sounded.

Opening his eyes, Travis glanced toward the house just in time to see the screen close behind Lindy's denim-clad derriere. Winning her back was definitely a prize worth working for, and no matter what level of hell Robertson put him through today, he would keep a tight rein on his pride.

"Just keep your mouth shut and get the job done," he ordered himself as he followed Robertson into the barn.

An hour later, Travis stuck his head under the lukewarm trickle of water flowing from the barn's small shower. Somehow he'd found the fortitude to do exactly as he'd promised himself, but it hadn't been easy. Robertson had barked out a few terse orders then left Travis alone with two smelly, stubborn cows standing on a thick carpet of manure and nasty hay. He'd been completely out of his element, but he'd gotten the job done.

Mucking out the stalls had been as disgusting and back-breaking as he'd feared, but after the first few minutes, his muscles had begun to warm, and while he didn't enjoy the chore, he did welcome the opportunity to work out his frustrations. Pummeling Robertson would have been more satisfying, but a man couldn't have everything he wanted.

What Travis really wanted—what he had to find a way to have—was Lindy. She was all that mattered, and if he had to, he'd put himself through another hundred and fifty mornings just like this one in order to earn her forgiveness.

Lindy hurried into the depths of the barn, intent on delivering the clean towels and change of clothes before Travis finished cleaning up. The lousy water pressure out here made it next to impossible to accomplish anything with a "quick" shower.

Passing the freshly cleaned stalls, she paused to admire Travis's handiwork. He might be a beginner, but he'd done a thorough job mucking out the stalls. Thelma and Louise contentedly munched hay, apparently pleased with his efforts.

Hearing the shower still running, Lindy praised her timing. She needed to sneak the towels and overalls into his range and get out of here. The very last thing she needed was to accidentally find herself in close quarters with a freshly showered, naked Travis. Lindy's hand trembled as she slid the pocket door aside. A naked back stretched between broad shoulders filled her vision.

"Oh, my," she exclaimed on a raspy sigh.

Travis crouched in front of the sink, probably searching for something to dry off with. The skin on his muscled tush rippled as he rose to his full height. He turned and calmly faced her in all his glory. And, dear God, what glory!

Rather than offering him the towel as cover, she clutched it to her chest, waiting for her breath to return. And blast him, he just stood there, utterly comfortable in his own skin. And why not? She'd spent plenty time wrapped in all that skin. She knew just how comfortable it was.

Travis closed the distance between them with a single step. "You're staring." His voice caressed her ears, stirring memories of long nights spent wrapped in Travis's arms, listening as he whispered erotic compliments.

"You're naked," she told him, her entire focus resting on his, uh, nakedness.

"I find showering—among other things—more effective when I'm naked."

Don't think about "other things," she ordered her brain. But it was no use. Visions of her own nakedness joined the images playing in her mind. Both hands dropped, limp, to her side, the towel and overalls landing in a heap at her feet.

Travis's gaze slid away from her face, traveling lower. Her nipples snapped to attention. She trembled as the sensitive flesh grazed the cotton of her bra. A salacious grin bloomed beneath the desire in his green-gold eyes.

A moan formed in her throat, and she clamped her teeth, locking the sound inside. Travis rubbed his forefinger across her lower lip. Lindy's lips parted upon contact and the moan trapped on the back of her tongue erupted.

He answered with a guttural moan of his own and stepped forward. His hands gripped her just above the elbows, then moved slowly, traveling to her shoulders, pulling her closer with every inch.

"God, Lindy. I need to kiss you."

His warm breath tickled her cheek. Her dormant desire exploded, turning her brain to mush. She couldn't think or speak. Her other senses kicked into overdrive as she yearned to taste him again. Her skin caught fire beneath his touch.

I need you, too.

Underneath the scent of soap, she could still smell him. Forget pheromones. Someone should bottle *Travis.* Her body moved of its own free will, sliding forward, slipping into him. His long, strong frame still fit her to a T.

Her head dropped back, her mouth fell open. Her heart seemed to stop beating, waiting for Travis's kiss to give it life again. Committed to the destiny of this first kiss after so many months of longing, her eyelids fluttered closed.

His lips brushed hers softly, the gentle caress a welcome home. A sigh of pleasure slipped from her and slid into the dark, warm recesses of Travis's mouth.

Somewhere near her feet, Travis's cell phone rang. She

stiffened. Why did her body respond so quickly to the one man her heart and her brain knew she couldn't trust?

Travis's arms banded more tightly around her back. "Don't worry," he whispered against her numb lips. "My voice mail will pick up. I'll deal with whoever it is after we deal with this."

His words stung like a slap to the face.

What was she doing? She couldn't let herself get sucked back in. She was just a temporary diversion. The voice in his mailbox, whoever it was, would pull him away from her. Again.

Closing her eyes, she jerked back, swallowing her pain and summoning her voice from the pit of her stomach. "We've got nothing left to deal with, Travis."

Travis hooked one ridiculous suspender over his bare shoulder before snatching the shrilling cell phone off the bathroom floor. He considered letting the call roll into voice mail again, but this was the fourth call in the five minutes since Lindy'd stormed off.

He opened the phone and checked the display. Out of area. No help there. *Everything* was out of area here. Glad the caller couldn't see him in Pops's hand-me-downs, he answered. "Monroe."

"Travis. Thank God." Grant's voice wobbled with what sounded like honest concern. "I was afraid you'd never pick up."

"I was in the shower." *Sort of.* "What's up?"

"Got a situation down here I need your help with."

Travis's fingers wrapped around the back of his neck, rubbing the knot throbbing there. "Who have you screwed with now, Grant?" He didn't bother to hide his aggravation.

"Just a little problem with the local authorities."

Damn. Grant had been in Mexico since the day after the Spring Fling. No telling how much trouble he could stir up down there. "Legitimate authorities?"

"Hell, yes! I know how to learn from my mistakes. It's all just a big misunderstanding."

"Big misunderstandings are your specialty. This is the third one in the last eighteen months." Travis paced the small bathroom, the cold tile against his bare feet doing little to douse his burning frustration. "Bottom line it for me. How much will it cost to make everyone understand?"

"Well, you know how complicated things are down here. You've gotta go through a lot of layers to smooth things out."

Yeah, he knew. South-of-the-border problem solving meant bribing every government official within a fifty-mile radius.

"Give me a number."

"Thirty grand." Grant's voice carried a hint of remorse, but it didn't ring true to Travis.

Christ! Grant's misunderstandings got more expensive every time. They'd already cost Travis a lot more than mere money.

"What have you gotten yourself mixed up with? No, forget it. I don't want to know. I'm not your babysitter anymore. Call your new girlfriend. I'm sure Julia's creative enough to get her hands on thirty grand."

"I'm not going to ask her for money."

"Call Dad then. He's got access to the same money and attorneys I do. Let him bail your ass out."

"Don't hassle me over this. We both know I screwed up. But this is the last time, I swear. It'll never happen again."

"I've heard that one before." He pressed his fingers against the tension settling between his eyes.

"We can't all be perfect like you, Travis. Just wire the freaking money."

Travis's anger snapped under the weight of a deathbed promise. "Damn it, Grant, if it weren't for Mom, I'd let your sorry carcass rot down there."

"You can't do that." Grant sighed, his cockiness replaced with anxiety. "I have to get out of here. Today."

He plopped onto the closed toilet seat, resting his throbbing head in his open palm. *Watch over them, Travis.*

I'm trying, Mom, but they make it so hard.

"The money'll be at your hotel within the hour, but I won't cover up a thirty-thousand-dollar mistake. You're going to have to come clean with Dad when you get home."

"Thanks, bro. I knew I could count on you."

As he ended the call and dialed his secretary, Lindy's voice rose up from his memory. *As long as you keep bailing him out, he'll keep getting into trouble.*

During their marriage, he'd made excuses for his younger brother's behavior, convinced Grant would eventually grow up and take responsibility for his own life. Now, he wasn't so sure.

She had always advocated tough love—a lesson obviously learned from her crafty grandfather—and after only a few hours of busting his butt to correct his own mistakes, Travis was beginning to see a method to Pops's madness.

Maybe, with luck, the next few months would improve the lives of the entire Monroe clan.

Chapter Six

Day eight of her ordeal dawned as deceptively bright and clear as had day seven. And day six. And every other blasted day since Pops had passed.

The sun kicked off from the eastern sky, marbling the cotton-ball clouds with swirls of cobalt-blue against a background of dusty-pink. The birds sang of their joy to be alive, free to soar through the treetops. The clean air carried the scent of spring.

Crossing the barnyard, Rufus at her heels as usual, Lindy blinked her gritty, sleep-deprived eyes and entered the barn without stopping to enjoy nature's grandeur.

She'd dawned cranky. And restless. And sad.

Despite working herself to the nubs every day, she couldn't remember her last full night's sleep. And she didn't know which bothered her most—her exhaustion or the wakeful hours spent thinking about the man sleeping down the hall.

At least sorrow kept her huddled in bed, facedown on a tear-dampened pillow. Her conflicted feelings for Travis had her wandering the house, pressing her ear to his door, hating the soft snoring sounds of deep sleep coming from the other side.

She'd become so muddled with exhaustion, last night she'd turned the knob, and when she'd found it unlocked, nearly allowed herself to slip inside. What she would have done on the other side of that door, she didn't know.

"Okay, so I have a pretty good idea," she admitted to Rufus. The dog plopped on his belly and rested his head on his paws, totally unimpressed with her truthfulness.

She humphed her disappointment at Rufus's lack of moral support and flipped on the meds room light. In addition to housing medical and nutritional supplies, this small space, barely bigger than a walk-in closet, housed a large animal scale and aluminum exam table for the vet's on-site visits. It was the one room Rufus never set paw in voluntarily.

Grabbing the milking stool, an industrial-size bottle of iodine, a pair of rubber surgical gloves and a soft rag, she headed for the stalls.

Thankfully self-preservation had kicked in last night. She'd released Travis's doorknob, tiptoed back to her own big, empty bed and recounted the seven hundred and eighty-three rose buds growing in her wallpaper.

Shaking off the image of being caged in by a trellis of fragile pink blooms, she situated her stool a few inches from Thelma's right side. Legs spread wide, Lindy lowered herself to the stool, careful to maintain contact with the large animal. Startling a fifteen-hundred-pound cow was a surefire way to get a few toes broken.

Meow.

Lindy felt the warmth of fluffy fur as Molly wended through her legs. "Hey, little momma. How're your babies this morning?"

Molly's golden eyes flicked to the hayloft overhead, as if checking for mischief. At only four weeks, the kittens weren't yet old enough to sneak down for a taste of fresh milk, but Molly never missed her chance. Neither did the proud papa, Milton, who waited atop Thelma's half wall.

She snapped her gloves into place before dousing the rag with iodine. The large beast tethered to a near-empty feeding trough heaved a sigh as Lindy ran the damp cloth over her full udder.

After a few fumbling misstarts, the sweet aroma of fresh, warm milk mingled with animal musk. It was a strangely homey smell.

She'd been raised on a farm, but until last month, Lindy had never milked a cow in her life. Lewis Family Farm was not a dairy operation, and maintaining a couple of heifers for familial dairy needs just wasn't cost-effective. But Thelma and her partner in crime, Louise, were vital to Lindy's plans. She'd created Country Daze to educate children about where the food on their plates and the clothes on their backs came from. It would be an awesome experience for children, and adults for that matter, who'd never seen anything more rural than the produce department at the grocery store.

Guests would pick fresh veggies, explore the barn,

churn butter, discover the rough, seedy texture of raw cotton and gasp over the enormous pigs and their adorable piglets. And what farm experience would be complete without hands-on milking demonstrations?

She emptied Thelma and repeated the process on Louise. Still a bit clumsy, her speed improved each time. Amazing how difficult it could be for a grown woman to accomplish something a hungry calf could manage mere minutes after birth.

Improved proficiency aside, Lindy couldn't afford to dawdle. Over the past four days, she'd established a routine for her morning chores that enabled her to clear out before Travis hit the barn. Since she wasn't sleeping, anyway, she slipped out of bed and started an hour earlier than usual. In addition to avoiding Travis, she'd hoped her revised schedule would exhaust her enough to allow for sleep. So far, no dice.

Outside, Red, the unimaginatively named rooster, began to crow. *Drat.* If she didn't hurry, she'd soon find herself in the very last place on earth she wanted to be. Alone with Travis.

Ever since Sunday morning's embarrassing scene in the barn, she'd managed to avoid Travis altogether. To her relief, she discovered that Alice made an excellent shield. Each time Travis entered Lindy's personal space, Alice popped up, threw a frown in his direction and poof, he was gone.

Like everyone else in town, Alice assumed the miscarriage had broken up her marriage. Lindy had never discussed the situation with anyone but Pops, too embarrassed to admit how low she'd ranked in her husband's life. No one else knew she'd packed up and snuck away in the night, leaving before her husband's mistress could kick her out.

Sometimes, pride outweighed honesty.

Red crowed again. Lindy jumped to her feet, hefting Louise's full pail and setting it next to its twin at the rear exit. The double doors at the barn's main entrance creaked open. She whipped off her used gloves and chucked them in the trash before hooking the stool with one grubby boot and skidding it into the meds room.

Promising herself she'd tidy up later when the barn was less populated, Lindy slapped off the light and slipped out the door facing the back porch just as the overhead lights went on in the main barn area.

"Whew. Too close," she muttered, looking down to gauge Rufus's reaction. But the dog, as ever present as her shadow, wasn't there.

Worried, she lifted the milk pails and slipped them through the porch railings, glad she'd taken the time to toss plastic covers over the pails. At least she wouldn't have to worry about cats and fresh milk while she coaxed Rufus out of his funk. That old dog mourned Pops every bit as much as she did.

Anxious to avoid Travis, Lindy crept back to the barn's rear entrance and peeked in. No Rufus. The occasional flick of Louise's tail was the only sign of life visible from this angle.

She skulked down the dimly lit hallway, past the meds room on her right. As she eased past the cramped bathroom to her left, she stumbled. This was the closest she'd been to the bathroom, aka the scene of the crime, in five days, and still the memory of what she'd almost allowed to happen shamed her.

Before she could berate herself yet again for almost

giving in to the temptation of Travis, she heard a familiar thump, thump, thumping as Rufus's tail smacked the straw-covered floor.

"That's the spot, huh, fella?" Travis's husky voice floated across the cavernous expanse.

Lindy felt his words all the way to her toes. What was it about this man? It was like he had some magical hold over her body. He didn't want her, would never be satisfied with what she had to offer, was only here out of guilt and obligation. Yet no matter how many times she repeated all the facts, her traitorous body still reacted.

Every. Blessed. Time.

Unable to resist, Lindy peeked around the corner. Travis's wide hand burrowed into the dog's thick brown fur. Rufus responded to Travis's touch with a groan of pure pleasure and rolled over, all four feet in the air, belly exposed, submitting completely.

God, but she envied that mutt.

Lindy bit into her lower lip to keep a groan of her own locked away. Traveling in reverse, she retraced her steps through the short hallway and back outside.

"Guess I don't have to worry about Rufus withering away from grief," she mumbled, retrieving the milk pails. Opening the screen with a stretched-out pinkie, she let herself into the mudroom, toed off her muddy boots and trudged into the kitchen.

Forget cranky, restless and sad. Rufus had sided with the enemy. Hurt jumped to the top of Lindy's emotional distress list.

"Must be the testosterone," she grumbled as she gingerly set the milk pails in the deep stainless steel kitchen sink. "Controls every male on the planet. Makes 'em all idiots."

Someone should institute an interplanetary commission where a gal could report infuriating testosterone-driven creatures. She pictured an army of Amazons dragging away the world's studliest males, leaving behind only easygoing menfolk, the ones best suited for a peaceful life of baby-making and jar opening.

Building up a head of steam, she twirled away from the sink and nearly plowed right into Alice.

"Whoa there, girl." Alice held freshly manicured fingers aloft. "Yesterday was my day at the Bunny Parlor. I can't have you messing up forty dollars' worth of store-bought beauty."

The Bunny Parlor, indeed. Harriet Kramer, former Miss Tennessee Cottontail, had chosen that gosh-awful name in the early sixties. Lindy always thought it sounded like a satellite location of Hugh Hefner's Playboy Club, rather than the weekly cut and set beauty salon it was.

Lindy closed her eyes for an extra long second, and pulled cinnamon-tinged air deep into her lungs.

So what if that stupid old dog wants to hang out with Travis? Those two faithless fleabags deserve each other.

She opened her eyes and let her breath out in a huff.

"Better?" Alice asked, one eyebrow hidden under her freshly curled hairdo. She'd make an excellent head Wonder Woman.

"I don't know." The scrape of wood on wood hollered through the kitchen as Lindy pulled out a heavy oak chair and plopped down at the table. "Rufus is hanging out with Travis." She clunked her elbows on the table and dropped her head into her hands. "Lord, Alice, I'm completely pathetic."

"Pish posh, girl. Your life's been turned on its ear. If you weren't a little overly emotional these days, then I'd be worried about you."

Lindy let her head slip lower, running her hands over her hair. Her eyes focused on the patterns scratched into the oak tabletop as she willed her tears back into their ducts. "Overly emotional sucks. I'm ready to snap out of it."

"When the time's right, I reckon you will. Until then, just take it one day at a time." Alice's hand covered Lindy's where they rested on her nape. "Remember, that which doesn't kill us makes us stronger."

Lifting her head, she turned and rested her cheek against Alice's softly rounded tummy. "Pops used to tell me that all the time." Her words disappeared in a hiccup.

As she sat there, soaking up the comfort of Alice's touch and her soothing litany of nonsense noises, Lindy realized how lucky she was to have this woman's support. Since Pops's death, she'd feared a lonely future. But she wasn't alone. She had Alice and Danny and his two precious little girls. And Shayna. And Chester.

And Travis, a little voice whispered inside her head.

No, not Travis. At least not forever.

Blocking out the confusion Travis brought to her mind, she burrowed deeper into Alice's hug, basking in the unconditional love, drawing on her strength.

Like Pops, Alice would always be there for her, offering hugs and kind words, and, when needed, a swift kick in the rear.

She had no idea how long she sat there and cried, but when she finally pulled back, Alice's apron was soaked. Lindy's head felt like someone had stuffed an extralarge bag of cotton balls through her ears. Her nose was running, her eyes ached and her throat was dry.

"Better?" Alice asked again, offering the handkerchief from her apron pocket. Lindy's tears had dampened the edges.

She blew her nose for all she was worth, surprised to discover she felt a hundred percent better. She felt like Strong Lewis Stock.

"Better." She rose to her feet, standing a few inches taller than this woman who was the closest thing she'd had to a mother in a very long time. Lindy kissed her powdery cheek, touched by the moisture pooling in Alice's eyes.

"Thanks. I feel stronger already."

If Pops were still alive, he'd begin kicking about now, telling her to remember him with pride and get on with the business of living. And that's just what she planned to do.

Travis heard the distinctive rumbling outside his bedroom window and cursed under his breath. What part of "scaling back my workload" had his father not understood? This was the fourth afternoon in a row the Federal Express truck had made the trek to Land's Cross.

"I hope they're charging the old man double." Pushing back from the folding table Alice had none-too-graciously provided as a temporary desk, Travis slowly stood. Gritting his teeth, he bit back a groan as his aching, overworked muscles begged to remain seated.

He wondered briefly just how much the driver would charge to hand carry today's delivery right to his desk. Whatever the cost, it'd be worth it to avoid the torture of the stairs.

The chime of the doorbell rang through the old house

and into his guest room–slash-office. If Monday, Tuesday and Wednesday were any indication, Alice wasn't going to answer it and offer to sign for his delivery.

Ignoring the pain shooting from his lumbar to his heels, he walked as upright as possible and greeted the young man who'd delivered his packages the past three days. At least today, his father had only sent two large envelopes, and the uniform-clad driver had carried them all the way to the porch.

Hallelujah, he wouldn't have to negotiate the porch steps. His calf muscles relaxed somewhat in gratitude. He signed the young man's electronic clipboard and returned it.

"Have a nice day." The young man turned the instant Travis had hold of the envelopes and skipped down the steps, sprinting all the way to his truck. A few days ago, Travis could've bounced down those steps, too. Had, as a matter of fact. But that was before he discovered muscles he felt certain the medical community knew nothing about.

As he watched the delivery truck's plume of dirt drift back toward the main road, he thought of all those years he'd awakened early each morning for a five-mile jog. He'd thought himself in decent shape. Then he'd volunteered to be a farmhand and discovered physically fit and fit for a day's hard labor were entirely different matters.

And didn't it sting to watch Lindy toss off a day's work without a single wrenched muscle? A week working the farm and he understood why she'd found it difficult to while away her days waiting for him to return from work. The undemanding life of the privileged did not suit her. Lindy thrived in this back-breaking world, carving life out of the land.

Filling his lungs with the fresh scent of clean air, he had to admit country life had its advantages. No smog, no crime, no traffic. Of course, no drive-through coffee service, no privacy, no twenty-four-hour local news. Hell, no twenty-four-hour anything.

A vivid red cardinal flew in from the side of the porch and touched down on the railing. Travis arched his back, stretching muscles refrozen in the five minutes he'd stood in one spot. His movement spooked the bird, who continued his flight across the porch and on toward the trees surrounding the duck pond, landing on an upside-down picnic table, right beside the one Lindy was sanding.

"Damn stubborn woman," Travis muttered. Tossing his paperwork onto the porch swing, he vaulted down the steps. Stubborn pride must be the antidote for hard farm work, because Travis forgot all about his sore muscles.

She makes me sign that stupid paper agreeing to pick up the slack in the workload, but won't ask for help. She's too busy trying to prove to the world she can do it all on her own.

If she wanted to sand picnic tables, then he was going to help her until the sun went down if necessary. And he didn't give a damn what his muscles had to say about it.

Lindy scraped the sanding block across the abused surface of the picnic table, exposing the fresh redwood planks hidden beneath several layers of mold and pine sap. Carefully following the grain, she worked with quick strokes, struggling to keep her focus on the here and now.

Forget the past. Scritch, scritch.
Don't agonize over the future. Scritch, scritch.
One day at a time.

She wadded her gummed-up piece of sandpaper and threw it toward the growing pile behind her. Exhaling a huff of breath through her sweat-sopped bangs, Lindy cut her eyes back to the house. But Travis no longer stood on the porch. That blasted dog at his feet, he stalked toward her, twin lines of agitation burrowed between his eyes.

What was bothering him? She tossed her sanding block on the table and stood, squaring her shoulders in his direction.

She fought the instinct to check her hair as she studied the fashion plate stalking in her direction. *He looks like he's off to play golf with the president.* His normally ruffled hair was combed neatly back from his freshly shaven face. A green polo shirt hugged his chest. Perfectly pleated chinos encased his long legs, their cuffed hems resting on highly polished leather loafers.

He looked, quite literally, like a million bucks. The shoes alone probably cost more than last month's feed bill.

You can take the man out of the cutthroat corporate world, but…

Travis had covered enough distance that she could see the temper brewing in his eyes. She clutched her empty hands at her breast, half expecting to find a scarlet *O* emblazoned across the placard of her overalls. *Obligation.* She hated that word.

The now familiar burn again singed the backs of her eyes. At least now she'd progressed to angry tears. She couldn't unleash her anger on the man at fault—Pops—so she settled for the man at present.

"You sure look pretty today," she singsonged. "Been to the Bunny Parlor?"

The iron set of his jaw didn't change, despite the flash of confusion that crossed his features. Of course he didn't understand. The Bunny Parlor was an inside joke, and everything about Travis shouted outsider.

"Never mind." Suddenly conscious of her eau de barnyard fragrance, her perpetually muddy boots and the thick layer of grime coating her body, she rounded the table. Unlike Travis, she hadn't stopped for a shower before lunch. Heck, she hadn't even stopped for lunch.

Travis moved a step closer, blocking her path. "What's going on here, Lindy?" His clean scent filled her nostrils.

She wanted to ignore him. Just push past his broad shoulders and get back to work, focusing all her thoughts on restoring the picnic tables. She wanted to think about anything but how good he smelled, how out of place he looked. How much he made her want.

Shifting her weight, she raised her chin, meeting his gaze head-on. "I'm working. That's what's going on here."

"According to your Ground Rules, I'm supposed to pick up the slack around here. I can't do that unless you ask for my help." His lips pressed into a tight line, as if forcefully locking the rest of his words inside. What was he trying so hard *not* to say?

"You're not dressed for this kind of work. Besides, didn't FedEx just drop off a load of important work only you could handle?" Looked like her inner bitch was making up for lost time.

"How many times do you want to have this same fight?" Every muscle in his body tensed, making him loom larger. "I've already told you, I'm scaling back my responsibilities at Monroe Enterprises. But apparently, you're not the only one who refuses to listen. That delivery was my father's idea of a power play. Sooner or later, he'll figure out my leave of absence this summer is no game."

He spun on his heel, nearly stepping on Rufus, who'd been laying at his feet, and rounded the table she'd been working on.

"What are you doing?" she asked as he pulled a sheet of sandpaper out of the packet.

"Don't you listen at all?" He glared at her, but Lindy wasn't sure how to respond. She'd listened to every word he'd said, but she still had no idea what was going on in his head.

Travis creased the full sheet of sandpaper down the middle then ripped it in two, setting one half aside and folding the other into a working square. "For the summer, my job is to help get this place ready for opening day, not play mind games with my father. *Or you.*" His lips pressed back into that word-trapping line as he began scrubbing his sandpaper across the table's abused surface.

Tiny flakes of redwood stain, sawdust and mold spores launched into the air before landing all over his *GQ* clothes. It seemed a pity to ruin such a sexy outfit.

"I'm not playing mind games. You've got your work to do and I've got mine."

"My work is to help you." He kept his face down and forced the words through clenched teeth.

"But you're not dressed for this kind of work. Go inside and deal with your paperwork."

"Quit worrying about my damned clothes," he roared, dropping the sandpaper and yanking his shirt over his head. The deep green material soared toward the pond, landing squarely on the legs of the overturned table she'd already finished sanding.

"Satisfied?"

Hardly, she thought as he turned his back on her and resumed his scrubbing. Any sassy comeback she may have thought up lodged in her throat. Despite the shade and the cooling breeze blowing across the pond, Lindy's body temp notched up several degrees as she watched the play of muscles across his back, the in and out of his rib cage, the flex of his buttocks.

Those look like high-dollar pants.

She quickly picked up her sanding block and fixed her eyes upon her working surface. But the *scritch* of Travis's steady strokes, the faint musk of working man, destroyed her concentration.

She peeked at Travis's fabulous hind end. He bent from the waist, putting his full weight behind each stroke, and the material cupped his posterior as if displaying a classic work of sculpture for her pleasure.

"Oh, drat." The shocking pain of a splinter wedged into her palm brought her art appreciation to an abrupt halt. She automatically brought her hand to her mouth, her teeth seeking the source of her distress.

She felt his body heat against her back before she heard him speak. "What happened?" His dusty hands gripped her upper arms, transferring more heat to her bare skin, and turned her to face him. He grasped her hand in his as carefully as he would a baby bird and turned it palm up. "Looks deep."

His thumb circled the wound, creating a pleasant tingling that overshadowed the ache. His eyes stayed locked on hers as he raised her palm, his thumb still anesthetizing her pain.

"Let me." When his lips touched her skin, Lindy balled her free hand into a fist. His teeth scraped the sensitive flesh of her palm. She winced, but didn't look away. He raised his eyebrows, seeking permission to proceed. She pressed her palm more snugly to his lips, silently accepting his aid.

Travis's lips brushed her palm again in what felt suspiciously like a kiss. Seconds later, he had the offending sliver of wood displayed on the tip of his finger.

"Got it." His voice had dropped another octave. The whirlpools in his eyes deepened, churning up the same emotion raging through Lindy's system.

Desire.

Standing before him, her own lips covering the same spot his had just vacated, Lindy searched her mind for a proper response—both to his words and his unspoken emotions.

Obligation.

The word splayed against her brain, dispelling the crazy sensual fog obscuring her logic. Proximity and convenience aside, Travis had no real interest in her. In a few months, he'd return to his world.

She had to make sure her heart didn't go with him.

Chapter Seven

As the sun arced high overhead, Lindy and Travis toiled in silence, performing the same job but working separately. She welcomed the heat, the dust, the monotonous drone of grit scraping wood. What she didn't welcome was the man working fiercely by her side.

How dare he accuse her of playing games when he was the one constantly changing the rules? Well, okay, so that wasn't exactly true. *She* had instituted the ground rules, but, sheesh, she hadn't expected him to actually follow them.

At the time, she'd been scared and angry and wanted to retain a smidgeon of control. She hadn't intended to draw Travis deeper into her life. How could she have guessed he'd end up working by her side, and half-naked to boot?

Having finished another tabletop, her third so far, she

tipped it over, exposing the less damaged underside. Trying to hide her confusion behind the labor, she lowered to her knees and kept right on working.

Despite Travis's claims of distancing himself from Monroe Enterprises, she'd expected the company and his family to monopolize his time. Lindy figured she and Travis would see very little of each other, just like those weeks following the accident. She never imagined Travis would actually pitch in around here, doing the dirty, back-breaking chores she and Danny had assigned him.

Placing a clean square of sandpaper on her block, she cringed, remembering the cruel initiation Travis had received that first morning. She and Danny had been pretty rough on him. Her conscience dinged her, making her feel even worse because Travis had never once complained.

Beside her, Travis tipped his third table over and started on the bottom. With his long arms, he worked faster than she did. The one-table lead she'd started with was gone.

Gnawing on her bottom lip as she worked, she put a hundred and ten percent of her focus into ignoring him and his muscular arms. Despite her best efforts, she failed miserably. She'd been hyperaware of him all afternoon.

On the plus side, they accomplished a remarkable amount of work. By late afternoon, eight out of ten tables were sanded and ready to paint.

"That old wood looks a thousand times better already." Alice's voice broke into the drone of their work as she strolled up, carrying a tray of iced tea and lemon squares. "I brought y'all a snack."

Lindy wiped her palms down her pant leg, but her overalls were covered in as much sawdust as her hands.

From the corner of her eye, she noticed Travis unraveling the water hose and dragging it in their direction.

"Thanks, Alice. I'm starved."

Travis pulled up short, his piercing green eyes burning straight through her. One sandy palm hovering over the spot warmed by his stare, she pivoted to the side, hoping to deflect the heat of his gaze.

"No wonder," Alice said, apparently unaware Lindy was about to burst into flames. "A body's not made to work through lunch."

Pulling the spray nozzle's trigger, Travis rinsed his hands before bending and raising the sprayer up, letting water rain down over his head. His wet hair, blacker than black under the afternoon sun, plastered to his head. Lindy swallowed, watching water sluice down his naked chest. He shook his head like a dog emerging from the pond and extended the hose.

Her fingers itched to smooth back his tousled hair, to pop the droplets shimmering in the southward-pointing arrow of soft dark hair across his chest. She yearned to touch him, just as she had less than a week ago in the barn shower. That thought, thankfully, brought reminders of Travis's priorities, of the cell phone that connected him to his overly dependent family.

Careful not to let her skin touch his, she took the hose, and lowered her eyes to his hips, hoping direct evidence of his cellular link would further bolster her defenses. But drat, no phone. Not even the incriminating belt clip.

Of course, he hadn't planned on working away from his desk this afternoon.

As she washed the dirt and dust from her hands and

arms, Travis took a glass from the tray and downed his tea in several long gulps. When he finished, he wiped his forearm across his mouth. "Thanks, Mrs. Robertson. That really hit the spot."

Lindy picked up the other glass, trying to ignore her heart's foolish flutter. She was such a sucker for good manners.

"I didn't do it for you, boy." Alice chuckled. "I gotta help you keep up your strength, elsewise Lindy'd have *me* out here melting under the hot sun."

Lindy nearly choked on her tea as she started to object, but Alice stopped her protests with a laugh.

"Don't have a conniption. You know I was only joking." Arms crossed over her chest, Alice studied Travis. "You really shouldn't be out here working in your church pants."

With a "tsk, tsk" in Travis's direction and a wave in Lindy's, Alice left the pitcher of tea behind and returned to the house.

Travis looked down at his pants, seeming to notice the dirt and grass-stained knees for the first time. "Guess you were right. I'm not dressed for this kind of work."

"Now you know why overalls are so popular around here."

"All this time, I just thought you were making a fashion statement." One corner of his mouth curled up as he retrieved his discarded shirt before plucking several lemon squares from the tray. "Be right back."

Lindy popped a lemon square in her mouth. She watched him hurry inside, his half smile tormenting her. This past week, she'd seen glimpses of the man she'd first fallen in love with, the man with a great sense of humor, the man she'd shared her dreams with, made a baby with.

Drawing in a ragged breath, she set her tea glass back

on the tray. She'd almost forgotten how much she liked that thoughtful, patient fella. What had he done with the unemotional business mogul she'd walked out on? And when would *that* guy show up again?

Across the yard, the front door clanged closed. Lindy picked up her sanding block again. Her conscience dinged her again, harder this time. She hadn't said one kind word to him since his arrival, despite all he'd done to help save her farm. Seemed she'd abandoned her own good manners these days.

Hearing his footsteps approach, she looked up, but her politely formed thank-you slipped off the tip of her tongue at the sight of him. A plain white undershirt, as snug as a second skin, was tucked into thigh-hugging old jeans with frayed hems.

Lindy hurriedly turned her attention away from the gorgeous man and back to the filthy table before he caught her drooling.

When he reached the work area, Travis pulled out fresh sandpaper and, without a word, got back to work. The companionable silence that engulfed them felt strangely intimate, as if they had a great deal of experience working in tandem. Of course, nothing was further from the truth. The only thing she and Travis had ever done together was make love.

Desperate to banish *that* image from her brain, Lindy launched into a speech. "See those big tires over there?" she asked, nodding her head in the direction of four mud-covered tractor tires leaning against the barn. "I'm going to turn them into tire swings."

Travis straightened, studying the worn rubber. Lindy's breath caught as she watched him, his gaze moving from the old tires to the trees surrounding the picnic area. Suddenly his approval seemed imperative.

"Sounds like a good idea. It'll be something out of the ordinary for your young guests to enjoy."

She smiled, releasing her breath in an audible rush. "I want a visit to Country Daze to be a memorable experience for *all* our guests."

"I've been wondering something," he said, returning his focus to her. "This is a farming community, right?"

"Yeah."

"Well, how are farm kids going to benefit from a field trip to a farm?"

Good question. And she had a good answer. "They won't. We're targeting the more metropolitan school districts in and around Knoxville, Johnson City. And now that the interstate's complete, Kingsport isn't out of the question."

"Kingsport? That's at least an hour away, isn't it?"

"Yes, but it'll be worth the drive. We'll teach tons of fun stuff, wear 'em out and they'll probably nap on the way back to school."

Travis nodded toward the picnic tables. "I guess the kids'll bring sack lunches?"

"Yep. Next year, I'll add more tables so we can accommodate more than two groups at a time. I'd like to expand and offer something for the local community, too. Open the place up for birthday parties, family reunions, maybe even church picnics so I can earn extra money on the weekends. And hopefully within five years, I'll be able to put in a real playground."

Hearing the excitement in her voice, she clamped her mouth shut and snuck a peek at Travis. He stood only a few feet away, his hair and clothes coated in sawdust, his lips and eyes crinkled in a full smile, giving off more wattage than the Fourth of July fireworks.

She swallowed the jumble of emotions lodged in her throat and lowered her eyes, giving her full attention to the final strokes on her fifth table. "I'm sure it all sounds silly to you," she mumbled.

"Not at all. You have a well-thought-out plan with achievable goals, and unlike most first-year businesses, you aren't starting out too big. I'm sure you'll be a huge success."

She rocked back onto her heels and flicked her eyes to his, astonished to find what looked like admiration radiating in the green-gold depths. For several long seconds, she allowed herself to drown in the warmth of his praise. It felt good, right somehow, discussing her plans with him again, the way they had when they were dating.

A memory flashed through her brain, an image of her, dressed in one of her nightshirts, carrying two steaming cups of coffee, smiling at a rumpled Travis still lying in their bed.

During the early weeks of their marriage, coffee in bed had become a ritual. They'd just be together and talk. Learning more about each other, discussing what the day ahead held, dreaming of their future.

Whatever happened to those two happy, hopeful people?

Lindy flinched, breaking her gaze away from Travis's. Reality had intruded on their utopia and changed them both forever. She couldn't let herself forget that those two people no longer existed.

That's what made moments like this so dangerous. Fighting her body's desire for this man was hard enough. If she allowed her heart to become involved, he'd squash her again. And without her grandfather's love and support, Lindy wasn't sure she'd be able to pull herself back together a second time.

Lindy's aching muscles cried out for a long soak in the tub, but she didn't dare risk being anywhere near the bathroom when Travis came upstairs. She settled for a hot shower, but no matter how hard she scrubbed, she couldn't cleanse herself of the emotions that coated her skin like sunburn.

With her green terry-cloth robe wrapped around her still-damp body, she stepped out of the steamy bathroom and raced down the hall to her room, every bit as confused, frustrated and unsure as she'd been when she fled from Travis ten minutes ago.

What was wrong with her lately? Ever since Travis's unexpected arrival, she'd flip-flopped between cold freeze and nuclear meltdown. If she didn't get control of herself, and soon, she'd never survive the remaining hundred and forty-six days until Travis returned to his real life.

She pulled on a light blue bra and panty set. Through the wall, she heard the shower start. A languid heat filled her center. She gripped the edge of the dresser and closed her eyes, watching breathlessly as visions of Travis standing naked in her shower played out across her eyelids. Her memory easily superimposed a naked version of herself, joining him under the shower's hot spray as she'd done many times before.

Her skin tingled as she imagined Travis's wide palms cupping her breasts.

"Mmm." The sound of her own moans brought the X-rated daydream to an abrupt end. She opened her eyes and faced her flushed reflection in the dresser mirror. Dear God, she needed to figure out a way to diffuse this tension between them.

That's easy. Just sleep with the guy and move on.

The hand pulling her jeans over her hips trembled at the audacity of her own suggestion. Could she do that? Could she really tuck her emotions out of the way and sleep with Travis simply for the pleasure of a sexual release?

Lindy pulled a comfy peach-colored knit top over her head and pondered the question. She knew for certain the idealistic girl she'd been when she first met Travis would never have been satisfied with a loveless affair, but what about the woman she'd become?

Deep in her heart, Lindy admitted to herself that she would never become the type of woman to be satisfied with a loveless relationship. But sometimes, you had to take what life offered and make do.

Again catching her reflection in the dresser mirror, she fluffed her wet curls and studied the woman staring back at her. Healthy color and fresh freckles stamped her cheeks, rewards for a hard day's work outside.

Her body had changed over the past year, mostly because the weight she'd gained during her ill-fated pregnancy had settled in different places. Her hips were wider, her waist smaller, her breasts fuller. The biggest change was in her eyes, where small lines fanned from the corner and a hard-won wisdom added a glint of strength that had been missing twelve months ago.

Yes, she thought, this woman could take her pleasures where she found them because she'd been forced to learn how to make life work on her own terms.

Feeling bold, she opted for a dash of color across her lips and a spritz of perfume. She thought briefly of exchanging her jeans for something sexier, but quickly swatted that idea aside. After all, when push came to shove, she couldn't be sure which Lindy would show up. The idealistic young girl who dreamed of happily-ever-after, or the jaded woman who desperately needed to get laid.

The old iron bed creaked as Travis rose onto his elbows. He rubbed his hands across tired eyes, certain he'd lost his mind. As usual, he'd been dreaming of Lindy. Or rather, tonight he'd been remembering: the way she palmed the sanding block, the mouthwatering curve of her hips as she leaned across the picnic tables, the sawdust clinging to her breasts as she straightened.

Hoping to calm his body's rampant excitement, he breathed deeply through his nose only to exhale in a huff of frustration. Tonight his dreams seemed so real, so intense, he could practically smell her. That uniquely Lindy scent, cool earth and warm sunshine, stirred his senses as if she lay beside him.

Keep dreaming, Monroe.

He shook his head, trying to erase the alluring image of his wife that plagued his imagination, and turned to study the moonlight flowing in through the window. A sharp pain twisted in his chest as his heart stalled.

In the moon's glow he saw her, sitting Indian-style in the overstuffed armchair, her nightshirt pulled down over her knees, her arms belted around her waist. The John Deere tractor emblazoned across her sleepwear caught his attention, drawing his focus to the way her nipples pierced the shirt.

Trying to redirect his thoughts, he rolled onto his back, scooting up against the cold iron panel of the antique headboard. Bending a leg, he tented the sheet over his lap and flicked on the bedside lamp, dispelling the intimate moonlight.

"What are you doing here?" she asked, her voice a tantalizing mixture of sex and petulance.

He lifted an eyebrow at the irony of her question, silently asking the same of her. After all, this *was* his room. However temporary.

"I told you. I don't want to see you lose the farm just because your grandfather got some crazy idea in his head."

Lindy's instinct to defend her grandfather flashed across her face, followed immediately by acceptance. Not even Lewis stubbornness could argue away the facts.

"I've made a lot of mistakes, Lindy. I don't want to make another. Next to Pops, this farm is the most important thing in your life, always has been. If a little of my time will ensure you don't lose anything else important to you, then I want to give you that. I owe it to you."

"You don't owe me anything. This shouldn't be your problem. Pops had no right to drag you into this." She stiffened her spine. Her proud nipples poked even higher.

Look her in the eyes, man, or you're a goner.

He shifted, careful not to de-tent the sheet, and moved his legs closer to center, leaving plenty of available bed space. Just in case she wanted to join him.

"Your grandfather loved you. That gave him the right."

"No, it didn't." Her head twitched from side to side. "We're adults. We make our own decisions."

"What happens if we make the wrong decisions?"

"Then we live with the consequences."

"What about making new decisions?" he countered.

Her brows wrinkled as she cocked her head, aiming her smoky-blue eyes right at him. She seemed to be looking within herself, as if seeking the answer to a different question.

"No matter what happens this summer, Travis, we can't change the past." She leaped out of the chair and went to the window, standing with her back to him, arms hanging listlessly by her sides. The moonlight filtering in through the window cast her body in silhouette, giving her a fragile look.

"I'm not talking about changing the past," he insisted. "I'm talking about accepting it. Learning to live with it. Moving on."

"I *want* to move on, but how can I? For the next five months, Pops's will has us stuck in limbo."

The restrained rage in her voice shocked him. Was she mad at the situation? Her grandfather? Or was it talking about their past that made her so angry?

"Well, since we're stuck here together, maybe we should honor the spirit of your grandfather's will and deal with the unfinished business between us." He held his breath and waited. Would his suggestion make things better? Or much, much worse?

Her shoulders raised and lowered as she drew in a breath and released it on a loud sigh. She turned slowly. Her eyes bore into him again and he got that strange feeling she was still looking for something deep within herself.

After several long heartbeats, she nodded, as though she'd found her answer. "I've been thinking the same thing."

Travis released his pent-up breath, grateful to hear less anger in her voice.

A mere five feet separated the windowsill from the bed, but Lindy made the most of the distance. She sauntered in his direction as if she had all night to make the trip. A wicked gleam lit her eyes, making Travis strangely nervous. By the time she reached the bedside, his arousal strained against the tented sheet.

The tip of her tongue flicked out, moistening lips curled into a smile first formed in the Garden of Eden. And perhaps for the first time, Travis understood the true meaning of temptation.

She ran one finger up the calf of his bent leg, stopping to draw lazy circles around his kneecap. "You've been driving me crazy since you got here. Making me want you, even though I know I shouldn't."

Her teasing touch on his knee turned insistent, pressing his leg down flat. His erection strained even higher. "The attraction between us has always been potent."

As if struck by lightning, her body flew from its relatively safe position at his bedside and landed intimately across his lap, her thighs locked down on either side of his hips.

His hands reached for her elbows to steady her, but she settled back on her heels, staring at him, her chest heaving as if she'd run a four-minute mile.

"For the past year, I've been able to exorcise all this…" She fluttered her hands between them. "This *tension* by working my butt off building Country Daze. But that's not enough anymore. Now that you're here, I can't stop wanting you."

He tried to jackknife to a sitting position where he'd be able to reach her mouth. Not kissing her was killing him. "Lindy—"

"No more talking." She swooped down, swallowing her name as it slipped from his lips. Her bold tongue flicked across his lower lip, demanding entrance. He thought he felt her hands tremble as she pressed her palms against his chest, slowly slipping them up and around his shoulders. His skin burned under her touch.

A desperate need for oxygen forced them to break the kiss. Their lungs heaved in rhythm. Her breasts bumped against his chest, and he could feel the spike of her hard nipples, just as he knew she could feel his hardness between her thighs.

Pushing against his chest, she levered herself up. Blond curls flared around her head and a full flush colored her cheeks. Her lips were swollen and wet from his kisses.

"Lindy." He tried again to tell her how she made him feel, but she cut him off, lowering her head again, those wild blond curls curtaining his face.

He struggled to keep up with her frenetic seduction. She'd taken him by surprise, but this powder keg of lust was just what he needed. He'd stored up twelve months of desire for this woman. It would probably take him a lifetime to use it up, but oh, man, what a way to spend a lifetime.

A growl that could have been hers or his filled the air as Lindy nipped his lower lip before lifting her head. She clutched the T-shirt's hem and yanked it up and over her head.

"Beautiful." His hands trembled as he skimmed them over her hips, up her rib cage to cup her breasts. She quivered, rocking intimately against his groin, bringing him dangerously close to the breaking point.

After weeks of waiting for Lindy's forgiveness, she'd finally taken the first step and come to him. Now they could work at healing the past. He opened his mouth to speak the words he'd dreamed of telling her for the past year, but she cut him off yet again.

"I was doing just fine till you got here. Now I'm completely out of control." She trailed her fingers down the center of his body, the touch made more powerful because she barely made contact. "I want you." The anger had returned to her voice.

"The emotions between us have always been too strong to resist."

"No emotions." Her right hand balled into a fist and lightly pounded his chest. "This is just sex, purely physical satisfaction. It won't change anything."

Her vicious tone struck deep inside him, wounding him in that vulnerable spot where his ego touched his heart. Despite everything he'd tried to show her, despite all the time that had passed, she still wasn't ready to admit she cared for him.

His anger rose, equaling hers. He shifted his hips, reversing their positions. As he rolled on top of her, the sheet pulled away from the mattress, remaining wedged between their naked bodies.

"Make no mistake, Lindy. *Everything* will change. No matter what we might want, nothing ever stays the same." He thought he saw fear spark in her eyes for a moment as she realized he once again stated facts she couldn't argue away.

Bracketing her wrists with one hand, he held them over her head. "You aren't the only one out of control here."

Uncertainty flashed in her eyes, but he stifled the urge to calm her fears and lowered his mouth, raining barely there kisses on her tender flesh. She arched her back, shimmied her shoulders, moving her breasts beneath his roving lips.

Her eyes begged him.

"More?" he asked.

She sucked her bottom lip into her mouth and nodded. Her figure might have changed, but her response to him had not. He knew her body's secrets, where she liked to be touched, how to trigger her release.

Shifting his weight forward, he stretched her arms even higher. The sheet wedged between them heightened the friction as he rocked his hips, grinding his erection against her center. With each forward thrust, he blew hot air across her straining nipples. Rock, press, blow. Rock, press, blow.

The tactic worked.

"Yeesss," she moaned as the orgasm hit her. Beneath his tense erection, her body quaked, nearly sending him over the edge, but he refused to follow. He wasn't finished yet.

Biting the inside of his cheek, he held tightly to his control and raised his head. A satisfied smile bloomed beneath her rosy cheeks, tempting him, testing his resolve to hold out for an emotional connection.

"Lindy, open your eyes."

Her lids fluttered open, her irises a thin blue ring around wide pupils. Doubling his determination, he pressed himself into her center once more. Her heavy lids dropped again.

"Look at me."

She raised erotic, slumberous eyes to his. "I see you."

Damn, he wanted this woman. But she'd raised the stakes. He couldn't afford to satisfy his physical need.

Using her stubborn pride against her, he pinned her to

the bed with a glare. Unless she took the coward's way out and closed her eyes, she would have no choice but to face him—and his words—head-on.

"I want to bury myself so deeply inside you you'll forget we're two different people."

She thrust her hips forward, upward. *"Yes."*

"But, as much as I want your body, I've discovered it isn't enough. Because sex *will* change everything. And if we give in to lust, we'll be cheating our hearts."

The satisfied smile slipped from her lips. "Damn it, leave our hearts out of this. We tried that. It doesn't work for us. We're too different. But we're good at this." She bucked beneath him. "Why deny us what we both want?"

"I'm not denying you anything. If a physical release was all you wanted, you'd be satisfied. But you're not, are you?"

Her lips parted and a sound escaped, half moan, half sigh. Her wrists strained against his hold.

"Admit you still have feelings for me, sweetheart, and I'll spend the next twenty-four hours making love to you," he promised before releasing her wrists.

She shoved against his chest, and he allowed himself to be pushed off her, onto his back. The mangled sheet rolled with him.

"I do have feelings for you," she railed. "I *was* feeling very turned on. Now I just feel pissed."

Nailing him with a look that would've turned a lesser man to mush, she flung her legs over the bed and stood, attempting to drag the sheet with her. To his perverted delight, his weight kept the fabric pinned to the bed, forcing Lindy to stand naked before him.

"Relax, sweetheart. I'm not looking for an undying

pledge of love and allegiance here. I just want to hear you admit there's more between us than phenomenal sex."

"What's wrong with phenomenal sex?" She propped her hand on her naked hip and his body screamed the same question.

Folding his arms behind his head, he allowed his eyes the pleasure of a long, leisurely look, taking in everything—her tangled hair, her swollen lips, her quivering stomach, her rock-hard calf muscles. "Nothing. But I want more."

The fury in her eyes burned a few thousand degrees hotter as she did a full-scale runway spin. His arousal ached, but he refused to jump like Pavlov's dog.

"Take a good look at what you turned down, Travis. My heart's off-limits, and you just lost your last chance at my body."

Chapter Eight

Admit you still have feelings for me.

Travis's words hung in the air like thick mountain mist, surrounding her, distorting her vision. As she stared across the pasture, she didn't see the verdant spring grass but rather the smoldering green-gold of Travis's eyes.

Remembering that heat, Lindy's hand trembled as she tossed out fistfuls of feed for chickens long since frightened back into the coop by her foul mood. Clucking her apologies, she forced herself to rein in her temper. No sense taking her anger out on the stock, especially when the object of her frustration strolled across the barnyard wearing a huge grin.

His boots carried the telltale evidence of his mucking chores. He obviously wasn't fresh from the bed, but darn it, did he have to look so relaxed and well-rested this morning?

She hadn't gotten a wink of sleep last night. Hadn't even bothered to try. Instead she'd taken her untapped energy and reorganized her office. She was bone tired and frustrated as all get-out this morning, but at least her desk was clean.

Somewhere between arranging her credit card statements in chronological order and updating the Material Safety Data Sheets on her pesticides, she'd decided the only way to survive this summer with her pride intact was to treat Travis like an employee. No more polite conversations at dinner. No more sharing of dreams or talk of the future. No more midnight visits to his room. No more contact whatsoever not directly related to Travis's agreement to help lighten her workload.

"Morning." Travis threaded his fingers into the six-foot wall of chicken wire and smiled as if they were bosom buddies.

The nerve of this man, acting like nothing happened. As if he hadn't totally rejected and humiliated her last night.

With the old Folgers can that served as her feed canister hugged to her chest, she turned her back. He didn't need to see the circles under her eyes or the deep lines exhaustion had carved along the edges of her mouth.

"I thought we might have a driving lesson this afternoon."

Still giving him her back, she shrugged her shoulders and released a noncommittal noise from the back of her throat. Time spent in an automobile's tight confines did not fit into her keep-it-professional plan.

"Of course, if you're too scared, I can understand."

Spinning around, she chucked a double handful of chicken feed at his feet. Dust stirred and settled, adding another layer of grime to his boots.

"I'm *not* scared." She paused to swallow, making sure to keep her voice screech-free. "I'm busy. Farming's not the kind of business where you can fax orders to a secretary and take the afternoon off for a little joyriding."

"Joyriding's not what I had in mind. If you're going to get over your panic attacks, I figure getting down the driveway and back will be an accomplishment for your first lesson."

She tilted her chin. "A blind man could handle that. I'm not handicapped, just—uncomfortable."

"Getting comfortable is the point of rule number seven."

"Well, I don't have time for rule number seven today."

"If I didn't know better, I'd think it wasn't getting in the car that makes you uncomfortable, but spending time with *me*."

Lindy lifted her chin, unable to resist such an obvious challenge. "I'll meet you on the driveway in thirty minutes."

Lindy eyed the metallic silver death trap and the *clean* man leaning against the fender. The light breeze blowing across the yard failed to ruffle his still-wet hair, and the sneakers beneath his crossed ankles were poop-free.

Suddenly her decision to sanitize Thelma and Louise's water trough rather than spend her thirty-minute reprieve showering and pulling on clean clothes seemed foolish rather than efficient. She'd given him the upper hand. Again.

Stopping a good six feet away, she crossed her arms over her chest and glared at him. "Okay, let's get this over with." She'd promised to try these driving lessons. Not once had she agreed to be pleasant.

Travis remained relaxed. "I've been thinking about the best approach for these lessons."

Should've known he'd have a plan. "Let's hear it." Feeling sticky and gritty, she took a small step closer.

The midmorning sun reflected in his mirrored shades as he stood to his full height. "Given your history, and the fact that you're able to drive that old truck when you have to, I think your fear stems from being in the passenger seat because the passenger has no control."

She made no comment, miffed that he'd nailed her problem in one guess. It took a lot of concentration, but she could force herself behind the wheel of Pops's big truck. But no matter how hard she concentrated, no matter how wimpy it made her feel, she couldn't get herself into a sedan. Every time she'd tried, horrible memories had swamped her, made her physically ill.

Her silence didn't seem to faze Travis. He continued as if he'd known she wouldn't speak.

"The logical first step is to become comfortable in a car again. The best way to do that is behind the wheel, where you'll feel a sense of control. Once you've done that, we'll move you to the passenger seat."

Lindy tried to swallow, but her throat felt parched. She kept her gaze pasted on the vehicle behind him. "Sounds like you have it all figured out."

"I've done a lot of thinking about how the accident changed your life." Travis's voice lowered, softening to a level designed to calm and comfort. "Thinking of how to take away your fear."

Her eyes darted to his face. The set of his jaw reflected his guilt, his rampaging obligation. Familiar disappointment burned through her gut like an ulcer. Was she forever destined to be a burden to this man?

She massaged her belly. "I hope your work didn't suffer."

Patience joined the emotional mix in his eyes. "Save your energy, Lindy. Picking a fight won't get you out of this."

He moved forward, opening the driver's-side door. The rich smell of leather and Travis wafted out. Before she could stop herself, she closed her eyes and drew in a deep breath, inhaling the tantalizing aroma that reminded her of good times. And bad.

He must have noticed the shiver that passed through her because he cupped her chin and raised her eyes to his. He'd removed his sunglasses, hooked them in the neck of his T-shirt.

"Relax, sweetheart. We're going to do this nice and slow. We've got all summer."

Relax, sweetheart. Those were the same words he'd thrown at her last night. Hearing them again snapped her anger back into place. "I know perfectly well how much longer you'll be here. Twenty weeks, five days."

"Plenty of time for you to get to the mailbox and back," he answered, unperturbed by her rudeness.

She jerked her chin, breaking his hold, and stepped around the open door. Close up, the smell intensified. She eyed the bucket seat, the nubbed leather steering wheel, the colorful BMW logo on the immaculate floor mats.

A gray fog began to creep into her vision. Her heart rate shifted into overdrive, every rapid beat pounding against her temples.

I can't do this.

She stepped back, crashing into Travis's solid chest. Her pulse echoed so loudly in her ears she feared he could hear it. She wanted to move out of earshot, but her only escape route was forward, directly into the mouth of the beast.

Turning, she wedged her stiff back against the car frame, folding her arms across her chest. Travis advanced, closing the narrow gap between them, and rested his hands on her shoulders. His fingers squeezed reassuringly as he bent his knees, looking up into her face. "Slow and easy." The calm green oasis of his eyes stayed level with hers as he squatted in front of her. "Take it one step at a time."

Even sitting sideways with her feet planted on solid ground, the leather cupped her bottom, giving her a comfy perch in her own personal hell.

"Let me go, Travis, before my boots get chicken poop all over the inside of your car." She canted forward, but he didn't budge. Their faces were aligned, so close that she inhaled his exhale, tasting the minty freshness of his toothpaste.

"You can do this, Lindy." The encouraging words fluttered over her ears. His fingers brushed the back of her right knee and she jumped, scraping her scalp on the door frame.

Travis tugged her dirty boot off. It thumped to the ground, followed quickly by her sock. Her toes wiggled in response to the cool air feathering over her foot.

She wanted to jump up, demand to know what the heck he was doing, say something nasty enough to light his temper, run for her life. But before she could move, he'd removed the boot and sock from her other foot.

"Slow and easy." His eyes never left her face. He placed her bare feet on the floorboard, then pushed against her knees until her body faced forward.

"The first step's always the hardest, but you don't

have to do it alone," he whispered before standing and closing the door.

Her bare toes curled around the brake pedal and her sweaty palms gripped the steering wheel at ten and two.

Like ghostly haunts, sounds from the past filtered out of her memory, floated front and center. Skidding tires, the crush of metal on metal, breaking glass, her screams.

That which doesn't kill us makes us stronger, Lindy girl.

Feeling the comfort of Pops's presence, she whispered, "I can do this."

Readjusting her slippery grip on the wheel, she ignored the sweat popping out on her forehead as Travis slid into the passenger seat. His wide shoulders and long legs ate up all the available breathing room inside the cab. She heard the jangle of keys from her right, but couldn't take her eyes off the speedometer. The orange pointer rested on the big white zero, offering her a measure of comfort.

"You're doing great, Lindy. Now we need to start the engine so we can roll down the windows." Travis's words barely penetrated the roar of blood rushing in her ears.

He slowly slipped the key into the ignition and turned it. The powerful engine roared to life, sending vibrations up through her feet, making her stomach flip-flop. The acrid taste of bile filled her mouth.

She fumbled for the door handle. "I have to get out of here." Her fingers found the cool metal tab and yanked, then pushed, flinging the door open. A rush of fresh air flowed over her heated cheeks. She gulped it down, feeling her stomach settle somewhat.

His fingers grazed her knee. "Lindy, wait."

Too late. She couldn't wait another second. "I have to get

out of here," she repeated before freeing herself from the car. She ran all the way to the house without looking back.

Leftover spaghetti churned in Lindy's stomach. For once, high-carb comfort food had failed to soothe her nerves. This morning's embarrassing scene with Travis still had her strung as tight as baling wire.

Unsettled, she tossed aside the book she wasn't reading and rose from the swing, crossing the porch to prop her hip against the railing and study Travis's car in the waning amber light of sunset. Tires, windshield, engine, bumpers, mirrors. So much the same as Pops's old truck, but for some reason, her brain didn't see it that way.

Drawn despite her fears, she left the security of the porch and approached the vehicle. Her uncontrollable panic attacks made her feel foolish and weak. She'd never forget the horrible day she'd discovered the embarrassing problem.

It was a week after her release from the hospital. Travis had, as usual, buried himself in his work, leaving her alone and lonely. To alleviate the depression she feared would never fade, she decided to return to school immediately. Graduation was only weeks away. Earning her degree became her driving ambition, the reason she got out of bed every day. School was the only thing left in her life she could control.

She'd tried to go to class, but the instant she'd climbed inside the fancy new car Travis had bought her, blackness had clouded her vision. Her heart rate had accelerated and her own screams had filled the cramped space. Desperate to escape, she'd accidentally locked herself in.

Her panic had escalated, overcoming her logic. She beat

against the door for what seemed like forever before unwittingly striking the unlock button. She flung open the door and fell to the ground, vomiting.

She hadn't been back inside a car since. Until this morning.

Trailing one finger along the vehicle's curves, she stopped at the driver's-side door. It wasn't really that complicated. Just lift the handle, open the door and slide in. Millions of people did it every day.

Clamping her eyes shut, Lindy reached out, her fingers probing the handle's cold metal, running the length before slipping underneath. She wanted to pull, to release the latch. But she couldn't.

She removed her hand and crossed her arms securely over her chest. She wasn't ready yet, but despite her cowardly desertion this morning, she'd taken a step in the right direction. And she hadn't done it alone.

From the moment he'd learned of her panic attacks, Travis had goaded her into facing her fear. If he hadn't added that infuriating rule seven to her list of Ground Rules, she might never have taken that first small step.

This afternoon she'd realized that she'd lost the excitement of jumping behind the wheel just to see where the road might take her. And she had become a prisoner of her fear.

Last fall, when the trees were aflame with autumn colors, she'd skipped the annual pilgrimage to Gatlinburg for the Great Smokey Mountain Harvest Festival and Fall Decorating. And last year, for the first time in twenty-six years, she'd missed the Noel Festival. Danny's oldest daughter, Shelley, had been crowned Junior Miss Noel, and Lindy hadn't been there to share the moment.

She would be there this year. Because Travis would

continue to push and prod until she had no fear left, until he'd checked rule number seven off the list.

She opened her eyes and sought his window. She knew he was up there. His blasted cell phone had pulled him away from the awkward silence of their dinner and he'd rushed upstairs to check his fax machine. Two hours later and he still hadn't come back downstairs.

That kind of doggedness was typical of Travis. He had his teeth sunk into something and he wouldn't quit, not until he'd solved the problem to his satisfaction.

A sudden shiver danced down her spine, and Lindy wished she could blame it on the cool evening breeze. Unfortunately the night air was uncommonly still. No, the shiver came from knowing he'd directed all that disciplined focus onto her. Travis wouldn't quit until he dealt with her to his satisfaction.

Suddenly his large frame filled the window. One hand held his cell glued to his ear and the other pinched the bridge of his nose. His hair was mussed and even from a distance, she could see his frown.

She trembled again, knowing Travis would suffer whatever personal sacrifices necessary to honor his obligations. The big question was, how long before his father and brother knocked her off the top of the list again?

Every muscle in Travis's body screamed for mercy. Sunburn stung the back of his neck, scratches crisscrossed his chest, and the yellow-green remains of a shiner colored half his ass.

He'd never felt better in his life.

After propping replacement bulbs for the cab-over lights

against the windshield, he dropped the engine oil cap in his pocket and climbed atop the tractor. His quads quivered from the effort. Even after two weeks of hard work, his muscles had yet to acclimate to farm life.

Shifting his weight to the balls of his feet, he balanced across the ancient John Deere's engine. Carefully leaning forward, he screwed the oil cap back into place amongst the tractor's hodgepodge engine. Rusty parts, probably original components, nested between shiny replacement parts. Plastic-insulated cables ran side by side with old wiring wrapped in black electrical tape.

Someone obviously kept this old gal running one repair at a time. The left side of his mouth curled up. Robertson damned sure wasn't the person in charge of tractor maintenance.

Yesterday morning, during the man's daily "just stopped by to make sure you were all right" inquisition, Lindy mentioned the tractor had started blowing smoke. Farmboy suggested she contact someone named Melvin to check it out.

Travis had bitten his tongue to keep from laughing out loud. Robertson might be an expert when it came to pig slop and crop fertilizer, but apparently, he didn't know squat about mechanics. Travis sure did. He'd been tinkering with engines since he was old enough to stare over the chauffeur's shoulder.

Eager to tackle a job without the handicap of inexperience, he'd volunteered immediately. It had taken him the entire afternoon to replace the exhaust manifold gasket. Today, he was concentrating on routine maintenance. Hot, messy work, but worth every uncomfortable second in exchange for contributing more than just menial labor around here.

Sweat trickled down his neck, soaking the collar of his shirt. Rising to his feet, he rolled his shoulders, working a kink out of his delts. His pride needed the boost of tackling a job he knew he could handle.

Nothing else was going according to plan around here.

He'd totally screwed his relationship with Lindy. What the hell had possessed him to pass up the opportunity to make love to her? He'd weighed his options and made a calculated decision: bruise her pride—temporarily. Win her heart—permanently.

What a freaking idiot!

And how did he follow that brilliant move? He pushed too hard with that damned driving lesson and scared the daylights out of her.

He popped off the five yellow lens covers spread across the tractor's cab. No wonder she'd barely spoken to him all week. And to top it all off, her lovesick neighbor found some excuse to show up every day. And the man always seemed to have his hands all over her. Hello hugs. Shoulder rubs. Goodbye kisses.

He'd promised himself he would ignore Robertson's transparent attempts to lure him into a fight, but every time Robertson touched Lindy, Travis felt his control slip, bringing his restraint closer to the breaking point.

Something had to give. And soon.

New bulbs in place, he snapped the lens covers back on. He needed some sign from Lindy that his efforts were paying off. Nothing huge. He'd be happy with something as simple as a kind word, maybe a "Thank you," or an "I'm really grateful for your help, Travis."

Noticing a loosened bolt in the light bar, he pulled a

wrench from his back pocket. But of course, she wasn't grateful. She hated him.

Feeling his frustrations rise, Travis overtightened the bolt, stripping it, making it useless. "Damn." The wrench slipped from his slick grip, bounced off the tractor's side and flopped to the ground a good six feet away from the rear tires.

"Hang on. I'll get that for you," Lindy called out from behind him.

He must've really been lost in his thoughts if she'd snuck up on him. Lately his radar was oversensitive when it came to his wife's whereabouts.

He squinted over the cab of the tractor, using his shirt-tail to wipe the perspiration from his eyes. "Uh, thanks. My hands are pretty greasy."

Dressed in faded denim cutoffs, a floppy hat and a dirt-smeared white T-shirt, Lindy rounded the tractor. She bent over to pick up the wrench, offering him a delicious rear view of her curves. A groan escaped through his clenched teeth.

His hands tingled with the need to touch her. She rose, wrench in hand, and turned to face him. He ground his left thumb into his right palm, trying to ease his desire.

"There're some extra gloves in the barn if your hands are bothering you."

Travis swallowed hard. Didn't she realize the only thing bothering him was her?

Tipping her head up, she handed him the wrench. The ugly old hat she wore did a lousy job of keeping the sun off her face. Rather than making her seem childlike, the fresh dusting of freckles across her nose turned her into the epitome of every man's farmer's-daughter fantasy.

"Thanks. Gloves are probably a good idea." He needed to put as many barriers between him and her skin as possible. He took the wrench, careful not to touch her with his oil-smeared hands.

"You're welcome." She rubbed her hands down her waist, tugging her damp shirt more snugly against her curves. "This old relic." She gave the tractor's tire an oddly affectionate kick. "Pops kept Ol' Bertha running on prayers and duct tape for years. Never could afford to replace her. Still can't."

Lindy paused, taking an extra deep breath. Travis watched her grapple with her grief. Why did she insist on hiding her emotions? He wanted to jump down and shake her, yell at her, anything to get her to open up, to trust him again. But that wasn't going to happen overnight. Hell, it might never happen.

"She just needs a little extra TLC," he answered, thinking as much about Lindy as the tractor. "You treat her right, and she'll stick with you for years yet."

Lindy flashed him a wobbly smile. "If you hadn't been here, I'd have to put my name at the bottom of Melvin Winstead's waiting list. He may be the best mechanic in town, but that man's the closest thing Tennessee has ever seen to a pirate."

"Glad to help. Feels good to be working with my hands again." He repocketed the wrench and held his greasy hands up.

Lindy squinted up at him, wiping sweat from her neck with her fingers, outlining her throat's curve with a trail of dirt. "You always were good with your hands."

She flushed and pulled her floppy hat farther down on

her face before picking up a basket of garden tools he hadn't noticed before. "Anyway, thanks."

Halfway to the barn, Lindy stopped and turned around, the basket clutched in both hands. "Not just for the tractor, Travis. For everything you've done around here."

Travis stood atop the tractor, jaw hanging open, watching her hips twitch as she hurried into the barn.

She's beginning to crack.

Chapter Nine

Lindy ducked inside the barn, welcoming the interior's cooler temperature against the flamelike heat in her cheeks.

Holy cow, that was one powerfully handsome man!

Spring sunshine had bronzed his skin and drawn character lines around his eyes, making him even sexier. And, heaven help her, when he raised his hands, memories of those blunt-tipped fingers skimming her breasts sent heat pooling between her thighs.

Walking to the corner of the barn where she stored her garden supplies, she tried to shake off the image of Travis's hands on her body. That line of thought would only lead her further into temptation.

Since her disastrous failed seduction last week, she'd avoided him, nursing her temper, hoping anger would douse her desire, but it hadn't worked. It had, in fac   back-fired. She wanted him more than ever.

Sighing, she returned her gardening tools to the proper shelves and crossed back to the wash basin near Thelma's and Louise's stalls.

Standing at the oversize industrial sink, she arched her back, stretching tired muscles. She loved tending the vegetable gardens, and she planned to reap much more than produce, she thought, lathering her hands and arms Country Daze would introduce hundreds of mostly city-bred children to the joy of taking seed and soil and growing something useful and delicious.

Recalling the stunned look on Travis's face following her awkward thanks, she rinsed the soap from her arms He'd played a big part in easing the workload, and she should've thanked him for his efforts long before today. His "free" labor was a godsend.

There was so much work involved with getting the farm up and running. No way she could've gotten everything done in time for opening day. Not working by herself

She'd considered hiring help earlier this spring, but had discarded the idea, afraid it would cause Pops to push himself too hard. Lionel Lewis's pride wouldn't stand for anyone thinking he was too weak to pull his own weight.

Her grandfather's stubborn streak had been legendary. She could've talked herself blue in the face, but he never would've understood it didn't make him less of a man to admit he couldn't do it all on his own anymore. There was no shame in letting those who loved him make things a bit easier for him.

Swallowing a sudden lump in her throat, she turned the

water off. Her thoughts about Pops sounded way too much like Travis's comments a few weeks ago at the reading of the will. He'd said she was unable to accept help as anything other than a sign of weakness. But he was wrong. Wasn't he?

She jerked a shop rag out of the bucket under the sink. Of course he was wrong. What about Alice? And Shayna?

Technically the two women were employees as well as friends. But Danny wasn't on the payroll, and he'd been helping around here since high school. Of course, he'd married her best friend, making him honorary family.

Lindy dropped the rag into the wash basin. Was Travis right? Was she really too stubborn for her own good? Was that why Pops felt he had to take such drastic measures to get her attention?

"Lindy! Lindy!" High-pitched voices floated on the late-afternoon breeze, blowing into the barn's dark corners like honeysuckle perfume on a hot June day. She grinned, grateful for the interruption. Now she could entertain her two favorite neighbors and postpone answering her own dangerous questions.

The minute she stepped from the barn, two little missiles wrapped themselves around her bare legs. She lowered her hands to their heads, both to welcome them and to steady them. If Danny's little girls continued their rocking, all three of them would end up in the dirt.

"Lindy! We found you!"

"You sure did, clever girls." She smiled down at Shelley and Tina Robertson, struck as always by how strongly they favored their mother. Straight brown hair the color of wet oak, glittering brown eyes and pug noses tipped toward the sky. Lindy felt the familiar twinge of sadness mixed with anger.

Her heart went out to these precious children whose mother had died too young. After three years, Lindy still missed her best friend. She silently renewed her promise to make sure these girls knew what a wonderful person Barb had been.

Well aware of her role in the children's game, she asked, "And now that you've found me, what are you going to do with me?"

"Oh, please, let me answer that one." Danny, who had strolled to a stop just outside the barn door, wiggled his eyebrows in classic villain fashion.

"Sure, Daddy. Tell Lindy about the party." Shelley, the oldest, smiled at her father.

"Party?" Lindy asked. "What's this about a party?"

"We're having a party for my birthday," Tina said. "With cake and ice cream and balloons and everything." Her eyes gleamed with visions of a party certain to turn the Queen of Hearts herself green with envy. "Go ahead, Daddy. Tell Lindy about the party."

"We're having a birthday party for Tina Saturday after next," Danny dutifully reported. "There'll be cake and ice cream and balloons and everything. Can you come?" His voice carried the same level of enthusiasm as his daughter's.

Lindy touched his shoulder in a show of support. She knew how hard celebrations were on him, but he never let his own emotions get in the way of his girls' happiness. He really was a great father. Barb would be so proud of him.

From his perch atop the tractor, Travis watched as Lindy turned to address the two brown-haired girls. Guilt again pressed heavy against his chest. She looked so natural surrounded by laughter and children.

Another man's children.

The pain in his chest seared straight through to his heart. From his vantage point, he had an eagle's-eye view of the group gathered in the barnyard. Watching the familylike scene sent a wave of acid into his stomach that made him nauseous. Robertson was so in love with Lindy it would've been funny if it didn't hurt so damn much.

Lindy stooped, getting eye to eye with the children. "I wouldn't miss such a fine party for all the chocolate milk in the world. In fact, I might even know where a girl could arrange for a hayride."

"A hayride? Really? Oh, Daddy, can we? Pleeeze."

"Pleeeze." With the childish belief that louder was better, the older sister joined in.

"We aren't really set up for a hayride at the house," Robertson answered.

"We can do it here if you'd like." Lindy sounded almost as excited as the children.

"Yea!" The two girls flung themselves at Lindy. All three females landed on their butts in the dirt. None of them appeared to mind a bit.

"Lindy, you don't know what you're saying. We're talking about twenty sugared-up little girls. It won't be pretty." Robertson might be playing the role of dutiful father, but it didn't seem to stop him from ogling Lindy's legs.

Travis couldn't stop his lips from peeling back from his teeth. Nor could he stop the low growl that slipped from his throat.

Lindy stood, shaking her hips as she wiped the dirt from her bottom. The move froze Travis in his tracks.

"Don't forget, I used to be a sugared-up little girl. I

know exactly what it's like. Besides, Barbara and I used to love hayrides."

"You and Momma used to have hayrides?" the sister's asked in unison.

"Yep. Every year on her birthday." She tweaked each girl on the nose. "Mine's in July, and it was always too hot. Your Momma's birthday was in October, perfect hayriding weather."

He recognized the look that crossed Robertson's face at the mention of his late wife. Travis understood the pain of losing your wife. He felt a pang of self-disgust as he thanked his lucky stars his loss wasn't as permanent as Dan's. He couldn't imagine a world without Lindy.

"But I thought the tractor was down again," Robertson said.

Travis buried his sympathy for Robertson as the man's gaze once again traveled the length of Lindy's legs. All's fair in love and war. And right now, his mechanical skills were the only appropriate weapon at his disposal.

Stepping away from the tractor, Travis spoke up for the first time. "It's running fine now."

Robertson's head snapped around. A guilty flush crept up from his neck as Farmboy realized Travis had witnessed his wandering eyes.

"Travis fixed it," Lindy said, tossing him a pleasant look that knocked his anger down several notches. "Took him less than two days. And he did it free of charge. Sure wouldn't have gotten that kind of service out of Melvin."

The note of courtesy in Lindy's voice offered Travis hope. She was definitely coming around.

Least he could do was meet her halfway. "I'll even chauffeur the hayride if you like."

"Who are you?" The older child eyed him with suspicion.

Travis bent his knees, aligning his face to hers. But he didn't adjust his voice. He'd always hated being talked down to.

"My name's Travis. Who are you?"

"Shelley Louise Robertson. I don't talk to strangers." The little girl had Lindy's chin lift down to an art.

Travis couldn't stop a smile from spreading across his face. "I'm not a stranger anymore. I just told you my name."

"Yeah, but I don't know you, so that makes you a stranger."

"True enough." He admired the young girl's confidence. Another trait picked up from Lindy, no doubt. "What would it take for us to be friends?"

"A grown-up we trust would have to say you were okay," her little sister piped up.

Travis straightened. Given the two grown-ups in attendance, he figured his odds of acceptance were pretty low.

"Shelley and Tina Robertson, I'd like you to meet Mr. Travis Monroe." Lindy's friendly introduction surprised him.

The smallest girl wrinkled her nose. "He's got your name, Lindy."

"Actually, little one, I've got his. Travis and I are married."

"Really?" Tina asked.

"Really."

"I didn't know you had a Mr. Lindy."

Lindy giggled, a charming blush covering her cheeks. "Tina, he's not Mr. Lindy."

"Where does he live?" the older sister demanded.

"He's been living in Atlanta, but he's going to live in

Land's Cross for a while. You girls can consider Travis a friend," Lindy told them. "I'll vouch for him."

"Vouch?" Shelley asked.

"That means I think he's okay." Lindy felt heat spread across her cheeks as Travis winked at her before heading back to the tractor.

"Cool," Shelley said, satisfied with Lindy's answer. "Can we go see the pigs?"

"Sure, baby." The second she granted permission, the girls pivoted and flew off. "Remember to keep all of your body parts outside the fence," Lindy yelled after them. You could never be too careful with your fingers and toes on a farm.

"Lindy, you didn't have to volunteer, but I sure am glad you did." Danny, who'd always been a demonstrative friend, draped an arm around her shoulders and hugged her to his side. Despite his smile, Lindy could feel his tension. He was worried about more than just the upcoming birthday party.

He sliced a frown over her shoulder. Lindy looked, too. Travis stood beside the tractor, fiddling with something behind the seat.

The animosity between the two men had grown as thick as buttermilk. She figured Danny felt a brotherly responsibility to protect her from Travis, but Danny needed to understand she didn't need his protection. After all, Travis was a pawn in Pops's scheme, too. He didn't have to be here, but he was. Lindy figured it was time they both eased up a little on Travis.

"I know I didn't have to, Danny. But I want to." Lindy smiled, watching the girls watching the pigs. "Besides, it's like seeing Barb and myself running around here. She always loved to come over and check on the stock when we were little."

"Little, hell." Danny smiled, obviously feeling a bit nostalgic himself. "She never outgrew that."

"No, she never did." Lindy stepped out of his loose embrace. Danny was too tall to talk to this close up. "Listen, not that I don't love your company, but what are you doing over here in the middle of the day? Who's minding the store?"

"Charlie's working part-time now that the time's changed. He says, 'More daylight hours mean more working hours.'"

Charlie Thompson was one of Pops's contemporaries. "I don't know where that generation gets its energy."

"Me, either, but I'm more than happy to help him work some of it off. And speaking of work, I came by to help you get the pumpkin seeds in."

"Already done." Lindy touched his arm to stop his progress toward the pen. "Danny, you know how much I appreciate all your help, but things are running pretty smooth around here now. Travis is getting the hang of things." She waved her hand in his direction. "We've got things under control. You've got your hands full with the Feed Store and—"

Her words ended abruptly as the shrill ring of Travis's cell phone disturbed the barnyard's calm. She cut her eyes to the side just as he lowered a red five-gallon gas container and pulled his cell free from his belt clip. He flipped the phone open and raised it to his ear. Mimicking the stance she'd witnessed the other night through his bedroom window, he pinched the bridge of his nose, a sure sign he was frustrated.

"It's no trouble for me to help out every now and again."

Danny's words barely penetrated her brain. Travis absorbed her attention as the hand covering his face skimmed his forehead and buried itself in his hair. Was he getting bad news?

Then Travis's jaw hardened and he jerked the phone from his ear and slammed it closed. He took two angry strides toward the house, stopped, pivoted, walked back to the gas can and replaced the cap.

Danny stepped forward and placed his hands on her upper arms, blocking Travis from her view. "That's what friends, especially good friends, are for." His voice carried a strange note today. Must be all the talk about Barb.

She heard the screen door slam and knew that Travis had returned to his office. *At least that darned company left him alone long enough for him to get the tractor running.*

Embarrassed by her ungracious thought, Lindy struggled to pick up the threads of her conversation with Danny. "Now and again is one thing. But if you keep pitching in on a daily basis, I'm going to have to start paying you. And I don't think either one of us would be comfortable with that."

"Lindy, I won't take your money," Danny sputtered, a familiar exasperation in his voice.

"Danny, I won't take your charity." She echoed his tone.

"Man, you're stubborn."

"That's what people keep telling me." And, God help her, she was beginning to think they might be right. "Now, if you'll keep those little angels out of my gardens while I clean up, y'all can stay for dinner and we'll plan the best five-year-old's birthday party in history."

Lindy sprinted through the mudroom, barely stopping long enough to toe off her gardening sneakers. She was every bit as excited about planning the upcoming birthday party as Shelley and Tina were. It would be like a trial run for Country Daze, a chance to see how the farm functioned with a large number of people milling about.

Grinning, she rushed into the kitchen and skidded to a halt.

"Yum." She took a big whiff and recognized the aroma of Alice's famous chicken and dumplings. Lindy's stomach growled as she crossed to the stove and lifted the pot lid. Licking her lips, she reached for the serving ladle nesting in the spoon rest, but a loud thunking noise directly overhead distracted her from nibbling.

Two more loud thunks. A door slam.

What in the world is going on up there?

She set the lid back on the pot and headed upstairs to investigate. Her bare feet touched down silently on the landing. Keeping her back against the wall, she slowly approached his room. Whatever had set him off must be really big. Travis hardly ever lost his temper.

The banging and slamming had stopped by the time she reached his doorway, and the silence was even more unsettling. She raised her hand to knock but the door suddenly flew open.

Travis stormed into the hallway. Lindy's raised fist bounced off his shoulder as he marched into her and sent her stumbling backward. He recovered quickly, dropping his suitcase so he could clutch her elbows to stabilize her.

"Owww!" She jumped out of his grasp and screamed as his suitcase landed on her naked toes.

Almost instantly, his large boot kicked the bag off her foot. "God, Lindy, I'm sorry."

"Darn, darn, darn." Hopping on one foot, she clutched

her stinging toes and tried to rub away the pain. "What've you got in that thing?"

Travis propped his fists at the waistband of his greasy, sweaty jeans and scowled at the lopsided leather suitcase. "I don't pack well when I'm mad."

"Pack?" Lindy lowered her foot back to the ground. Suddenly the pain in her toes was the least of her worries. She stared at him, taking in the clean yet unbuttoned shirt, its collar rolled under on one side, worn over a dirty T-shirt. An oil smear streaked across his right cheek. "You're leaving? Right now?"

"Yeah, got a problem with one of my projects. I've called an emergency board meeting for first thing in the morning."

"Sounds serious."

"One of our financial backers is threatening to pull out because of some stupid stunt Grant pulled." He threaded his fingers through his hair, the way he always did when his plans were thwarted. "Tanner just needs a little schmoozing, a goodwill gesture from Monroe Enterprises to remind him why he became involved in this project to begin with."

Lindy curled her lip. For such an intelligent man, Travis was a complete sucker when it came to dealing with his family, especially his good-for-nothing younger brother.

"So you're just going to rush off and soothe everyone's ruffled feathers?" She wagged her finger in his face. "If *Grant* offended this guy, shouldn't it be *Grant's* responsibility to apologize? When are you going to realize that as long as you keep cleaning up behind him, he'll never change?"

"Believe me, Lindy, I'd love nothing more than to let Grant figure a way out of this mess, but this project is too important. Hundreds of people's jobs hang in the balance." The fingers of his right hand pressed against the lines channeling between his brows. "I can't afford to teach Grant a lesson at the expense of Monroe Enterprises' employees."

"No, I guess you can't." Lindy struggled for a moment with the urge to add her own fingers to those massaging his brow. What a pickle. For the first time, she realized that Travis's rushing off to rescue his brother may have actually had very little to do with Grant. "How long will you be gone?"

"I'm not sure. The project can't afford to be shut down at this stage. It's the beginning of May already. If the work gets off schedule, the bricklayers will be pushed back to July and I'll have to pay time and a half to meet my move-in date."

"If you're gone more than three nights…" Her words trailed off. *I'll lose the farm.*

"I won't be gone that long." He moved forward, practically pinning her against the wall. It felt like the hallway, the house—the whole world—was shrinking as his musky male scent filled her brain. "I told you, I'm yours until the terms of the will are settled, sweetheart."

"Don't call me sweetheart," she ordered, her voice a feeble whisper as she pressed herself against the wall. Somehow, the distance between their bodies remained the same. Close. Too close.

"How about a goodbye kiss?" His index finger brushed a stray curl off her forehead and behind her ear.

His handsome face dangled near hers. She knew he was toying with her, but she was still extremely tempted. Resisting this man became harder and harder with each passing day.

His finger circled her lobe and trailed along her jaw to

her chin. Exerting the gentlest of pressure, he tilted her chin, forcing her to meet his stare.

She swallowed hard. Her lower lip dropped slightly.

Then the front door banged open as Shelley and Tina thundered into the house. Startled, Lindy snapped her head back, smacking it against the wall.

"Lindy! Ready or not, here we come," Danny called from downstairs.

Travis straightened, his mouth pressed into a grim line. "Sounds like my sudden departure plays right into his plans."

"What does that mean?"

He laughed harshly. "Robertson's bending over backward to offer you a perfect little ready-made family. Only thing left for him to do is to paint his name on your mailbox."

"That's ridiculous. Danny doesn't see us as a family. He's still in love with his wife."

"How long has his wife been dead?"

"Nearly three years."

"And you don't think that after three years the man is ready to move on, find another woman to help raise his children? A warm body to hold during the night?"

Lindy absently reached up to rub the sore spot where her skull had connected with the wall. "Probably, but—"

"But nothing. Ignoring his feelings won't make them go away." Travis bent to retrieve his suitcase then turned and headed downstairs.

Lindy followed, her mind grappling with the idea that Danny Robertson would think of her *that* way. No way. Not Danny. Heck, they'd been blood "brothers" since the age of five.

"You're wrong, Travis."

They reached the bottom of the stairs. The homey sounds of little-girl voices and rattling dishes drifted down the hallway. Travis laid his suitcase by the front door and took her elbow, leading her to the kitchen doorway.

The girls were setting the table. Danny was pouring four large glasses of milk. Lindy had to admit, they painted a lovely picture.

"Do you really believe that man's not trying to insinuate himself into your life? Your bed?" Travis whispered the words into Lindy's ear before dropping her elbow.

She turned her back on the cozy scene and looked up into her husband's serious face. She wanted to deny his words, but now that he'd planted the seed, the idea began to take root, offering a very different explanation for Danny's recent unusual behavior. Suddenly unsure of everything, she shrugged.

They stood silently staring into each other's eyes for a long moment. Lindy wondered if he was waiting for a better answer. Finally he leaned his face down level with hers and caressed his warm fingers down her cheek.

"Try not to miss me too much while I'm gone." His breath fanned across her lips, his taste lingering there.

He slipped out the front door before Lindy could respond. The sound of his engine roaring to life filtered into the front hall, and of course, since Travis was no longer within earshot, the perfect response danced through her brain.

I'm sure I won't even notice you're gone.

But of course, she knew the words were a lie.

Travis had once again taken up residence deep in her life, her thoughts. So deep, in fact, that despite the happy crowd waiting for her in the kitchen, her home already felt empty without him.

* * *

Five hours into the drive back to Land's Cross, Travis finally unknotted his tie. As he reached the fringes of the Great Smokey Mountains, his tense muscles began to relax. He lifted his fingers from the steering wheel and flexed them, releasing some of the stress he'd carried for the past sixty hours or so.

It had taken him two full days and an extra breakfast meeting to soothe Burt Tanner's ruffled feathers, but the downtown renovation project was back on track. The rest of his life, however, felt like a giant train wreck.

After less than a month of dealing with Winston's power plays, Marge had threatened to quit. Travis had offered her a disgustingly large raise and begged her to stay till September.

Travis grimaced and cranked up the car's air-conditioning. She'd really made him sweat, forcing him to wait and worry for two days before accepting his offer. During that time, Burt Tanner had insisted on a full audit of the project. The angry banker had questioned every expense, demanded justification for every decision from hiring practices to vendor selection.

Throughout the entire painful process, Susan, Tanner's "independent" auditor, sat quietly by her father's side, a miserable, apologetic expression on her pale face. Travis felt almost as bad for her as he did for himself.

The poor girl cringed every time her blustering father mentioned the fact that Grant had escorted Susan to the Spring Fling then ignored her the entire time. Travis wanted to throttle his damn fool brother who, according to the gossip mill, had spent the evening engaging in various lewd displays of public affection with Julia Wellborne while Susan sat alone.

Travis lowered his visor to block out the blazing sunset

as he continued driving northeast. Of course, Grant was no help at all. Travis wholeheartedly agreed with Lindy's assessment that Grant owed the Tanners a personal apology, but in typical fashion, Grant had left town.

So, he'd apologized on his brother's behalf and wined and dined the Tanners until his American Express card screamed for mercy. He'd hated every second of it, but as president of Monroe Enterprises, he was responsible for the reputation of the company and the security of its employees. Dealing with Grant's crap was an unfortunate added duty that came along with the job.

The ache in his fingers alerted him to his rising temper. He repeated his finger-wiggling exercise then lowered the driver's-side window, drawing in several deep breaths of clean, fresh air. The smell of flowers and sunshine filled his car, reminding him of Lindy. His foot pressed harder on the accelerator. Lindy and the farm were less than an hour away.

Staring down the vacant two-lane highway, Travis noticed a large red and white For Sale sign on the left-hand shoulder. Even though he was anxious to return to the farm, the developer in him couldn't resist the sign's lure.

Where other men got excited over stock tips or line scores, his thing was real estate. It was more than just the potential for profits. For him, the rush came from finding a new usefulness for a property deemed "outmoded."

He drove closer and realized the sign sat in front of an old abandoned warehouse. The four-story building looked like some kind of processing plant. The skeletal remains of a silo stood behind the main structure, and as he passed, he noted three large bay doors in his rearview mirror.

He braked, stopping in the middle of the road. This was

the first time he'd made this trip during the day, so he'd never noticed the warehouse before. Putting the Beemer in Reverse, he backed down the road and parked on the shoulder. He jumped out and stared at this anomaly.

Other than the dilapidated silo, the site looked like dozens of others he'd purchased in downtrodden urban areas. The full afternoon sun reflected in broken windows, making it shimmer like a mirage, as if his imagination had conjured the warehouse out of thin air.

He crossed the ditch and strolled to the corner of the fence line surrounding the property. According to the No Trespassing warning, the building used to be the Holcombe County Co-op. His mind whirled with possibilities. Taking full strides, he walked the length of the fence line, estimating the property's width. Two hundred yards. The lot looked to be twice as deep.

Out on the highway, a semitruck breezed by, honking as it passed. Travis raised his hand without taking his attention off the building. This property intrigued him. Its moderate size and unique location had to be ideal for something. All he had to do was figure out what that something was.

Whistling, he unclipped his phone and turned back toward his car. Stopping in front of the large real estate sign, he pushed the shortcut keys for his attorney's office.

There was nothing like the thrill of starting a new project. He felt as excited as Lindy had looked the afternoon she'd told him about her plans for Country Daze. A picture of his wife, dirty and sweaty and grinning, popped into his mind.

A warm female voice interrupted his thoughts. "Bradley Middleton's office. How may I help you?"

Travis smiled at the sound of the unfamiliar voice. Guess Brad finally fired poor lovesick Connie. "This is Travis Monroe. Is Brad in?"

"Yes, Mr. Monroe. Please hold while I connect you." Strains of Mozart replaced the woman's voice. Travis grinned, wondering how long before Connie's replacement fell for the boss.

"Travis, you old dog," Brad boomed into the phone a few seconds later. "Have you returned to the civilized world?"

"Not exactly. Look, I need a favor."

"Let me guess. Grant screwed up again."

"Actually, yeah, but this has nothing to do with him." Travis filled Brad in on the empty warehouse.

"Sounds intriguing, but I think you need a real estate agent, not a lawyer."

"If I contact my agent, every investor in a four-state area will know about this place, but if you make a few discreet inquiries, it'll remain under the radar."

"Are you going to cut me in on the profits?"

"What if there aren't any profits?"

"If you're involved, there'll be plenty of profits. Everything you touch comes out golden."

Travis thought about Lindy's angry face when she'd told him she didn't want him in Land's Cross. "Not everything, buddy."

In fact, lately, everything he touched turned angry. And everything he wanted kept moving further out of his reach.

Chapter Ten

Lindy poked a sticky finger into her mouth and swallowed the last of the frosting before encasing the freshly iced birthday cake in Tupperware. Licking the sweetness from her lips, she surveyed the crowd of sugared-up little girls. Tina and her guests zigzagged through the crowd, chasing Milton, the barn cat. They'd already exhausted poor Rufus.

Across the yard, in the pine grove near the pond, Travis and Danny, both wearing stern expressions, wrestled with a giant pink shoe-shaped piñata. The animosity between the two men seemed to have reached a stalemate, perhaps due to Danny's less frequent visits. Or, more likely, the fellas were acting like grown-ups for the children's sake.

Lindy didn't question the ceasefire, just gave thanks and hoped it held throughout the party.

Dipping a pink napkin into the ice chest under the picnic table, Lindy washed the remaining sugar from her fingers. A whirl of movement snagged her attention. She sucked in a quick breath as the stampeding children almost trampled poor Lucy Carstairs, who, at nearly nine months pregnant, moved too slowly to get out of the girls' path. Fortunately Lucy's husband, Junior, tugged her out of harm's way. A lump blocked Lindy's air pipe as Junior placed his palms over his wife's distended tummy.

Lindy's eyes watered as she turned her back on the tender scene. She'd known today would be difficult. When she'd stepped in two weeks ago and volunteered to host, she hadn't realized what day the party would fall on. Tina's birthday was next Tuesday, the eighteenth. But today was the fifteenth. The one-year anniversary of her miscarriage.

Did Travis remember?

Probably not. Dates and remembrances were his secretary's job. Even if he did recall today's significance, she doubted he'd mention it. No one ever spoke of the baby she'd lost. Not within her earshot, at least.

Sniffing back her tears, refusing to let them fall, Lindy tossed her dirty napkin at a nearby trash can. She missed. As she watched the wet tissue drop to the ground, several teardrops escaped, their warm wetness trickling down her face.

Squatting to retrieve her napkin, Lindy surreptitiously wiped her damp chin against her shoulders. She sucked in several deep breaths, exhaling through her mouth until her tears subsided. Today was a day for celebrating, not wallowing in self-pity. Grasping the napkin, Lindy stood and tossed it into the trash, along with her sadness.

Turning back to the table, Lindy scanned the gathering

and breathed a silent sigh to see everyone just as she'd left them. Her little pity party seemed to go unnoticed by the fifty or so guests milling comfortably around the picnic area.

The rural neighbors of Holcombe County didn't get many chances to congregate, so when an occasion arose, whole families turned out. Rather than a simple two-hour affair, Tina's birthday party had morphed into an all-day mini town picnic.

The adult guests congregated around the horseshoe stakes Travis had set up earlier, catching up on local gossip. And from the sideways looks the group bounced between her and Travis, Lindy knew her personal life was the hottest topic going these days.

Earlier, as she passed a tray of lemonade and brownies among the crowd clustered in lawn chairs near the pond, the grandparents in attendance didn't bother to hide their curiosity. Or their opinions.

"You planning on moving back to Atlanta with that husband of yours?"

"Is that city slicker you married gonna stick around and do right by you?"

"A woman could forgive a hunk like that anything."

"A man that handsome's nothing but trouble."

The over-sixty set weren't alone in their appreciation of Travis's good looks. The only women under the age of forty not sporting new sundresses and full makeup today were Lucy Carstairs and Lindy herself.

She tucked her blouse more neatly into her jeans as her gaze circled the barnyard, searching for Travis's tall form. She found him, still under the large pine tree, where he and Danny struggled to hang the piñata. Lindy noted the heavy-duty tack rope now tied to the paper shoe in place of the thin cord she'd attached earlier.

Was it too heavy? Had she stuffed in too much candy?

Watching as Danny bent his knees and, with Travis's help, hefted the piñata, she thought maybe she had. But she'd wanted to make sure all the children got plenty of loot.

Travis lifted the large knot at the other end of the thick rope. Worries over candy and overstuffed piñatas fled Lindy's mind. Beneath his stark white T-shirt, Travis's tanned muscles bunched as he reared back, prepared to toss the sling over the lowest tree branch.

Oh, my. Lindy suddenly wished she'd taken time for a new dress and some makeup.

Quickly busying herself wiping down the vinyl table-cloth, Lindy lowered her head. From beneath her lashes, she watched Travis make a perfect pitch. The long rope sailed over the branch on the first shot. Unfortunately the knot thudded against the center of Danny's back and bounced off. Danny released the piñata and turned to catch the rope before it could hit him a second time. The paper shoe hit the ground. The rope recoiled, zinging back over the branch.

Lindy abandoned all subtlety and raised her head, staring openly at the comedy of errors. *Ah, masculine bonding. Just what those two need.*

As the rope's full length landed atop the fallen shoe, both men glared at each other. Their formerly stern expressions turned downright menacing.

Or maybe not.

With great fanfare, Tina and Shelley raced to their daddy's side. The little girls' arms gestured between the tree, the piñata and the two adults, obviously offering instruction on the proper way to get the job done.

Lindy breathed a relieved sigh when Danny and Travis both stepped back. Rearranging their faces into less violent expressions, the two men stared at the wad of pink papier-mâché like a couple of pouty children.

A snicker started deep in Lindy's chest. By the time it broke free, it had grown to a full belly laugh, complete with a stitch in her side and tears in her eyes. When the pink shoe finally dangled securely from the tree, her laughter had calmed to chuckles. She pressed her fist into her still-twitching rib cage. When was the last time she'd laughed so hard?

A smidgen of peace settled into her heart, brightening a corner too long darkened by grief. Amazing what a good laugh will do for the soul.

Several hours later, Lindy's emotions were playing tug-of-war again as she rested beneath a maple tree before spearheading the day's final event: the hayride.

She wore a smile as she watched Tina and Shelley enjoy themselves. But deep down, she couldn't quite lock away the sadness of losing her son. The joy of this day seemed to highlight her loss, no matter how hard she fought the depressing feelings.

During the past year, she'd ignored her dream of motherhood while getting Country Daze up and running, but Travis's presence was pushing that dream to the forefront again. She couldn't picture herself having another man's child. But she knew happily-ever-after wasn't in store for her and Travis.

Nope. Stop. Don't go there. Not now.

Her throat already felt raw from the strain of swallowing tears all day. The last thing she needed were more sad thoughts to fight off. With her knees pulled to her chest, she wrapped her arms around her legs and wished she'd grabbed a glass of lemonade before seeking a moment alone under the tree.

Suddenly a moisture-beaded glass dangled in front of her. Her eyes tracked up the muscular arm proffering the beverage. When she connected with Travis's eyes, she saw sadness in the green-gold depths.

"Mind if I join you?"

Lindy accepted the lemonade and inclined her head. "Sure. I was just letting my hot dog settle before the hayride." She folded her legs Indian-style and leaned against the tree, feeling somehow grounded by the rough bark biting into her back.

"Good idea. Especially for all those kids. I didn't know little girls could eat like that."

Lindy chuckled. "Growing girls have big appetites, just like growing boys. They don't start worrying about their weight until they become teenagers."

Travis nodded, but the seriousness of his expression didn't match the lightness of their conversation. "How're you holding up?"

Lindy's shoulders straightened, pulling away from the tree. "Fine. The party's going well, don't you think?"

He took her hand, his strong fingers threading through hers. "I'm not talking about the party."

He remembered. Lindy felt a warm flutter around her heart.

"I know. I'm fine." She gulped her lemonade and wondered how *he* was holding up. If she voiced the question, would Travis be more honest with his answer than she'd been with hers?

A boisterous laugh broke into Lindy's thoughts. She turned to find the source and saw Chester, huddled with Edith Beaumont, flashing a huge grin their way.

"We're the hot topic today." A hint of annoyance tinged Travis's voice as he dropped her hand. "Mrs. Beaumont over there lectured me about our 'modern' marriage."

"Be glad you got the lecture and not the embarrassing marital advice."

"Like what?"

Lindy felt her face flame up. "Never mind." She'd never be able to look the little old lady in the eye again, not after enduring ten long minutes of graphic advice about keeping your man satisfied.

"Are these people always this free with their thoughts?"

"This is a small community. Things are different here. Everyone knows everyone else. And everyone cares."

Unlike the impersonal distance people impose in a large city. The words went unspoken, but a shadow of understanding darkened Travis's face as he drained his lemonade, then cleared his throat. "No sense adding any more fuel to the gossip mill."

Lindy suddenly realized what they must look like, sitting off to themselves, sharing a quiet glass of lemonade. A happily married couple. Just the opposite of reality.

"You catch on quick, Travis."

"Small towns don't have a corner on the gossip market."

Goodness knew she'd learned that the hard way. But good-natured speculation about much-loved neighbors was a far cry from the vicious rumors floating around some of those Atlanta cocktail parties Travis had dragged her to.

Before she could answer, Tina flew across the yard, Shelley running behind her, and flopped into Lindy's lap, brandishing a bright purple pig.

"Lindy, lookie what Shayna gave me." She yanked a string growing from the pig's tummy, and a series of mechanical oinks filled the air. The little girls clutched their bellies and fell to the ground giggling.

Over the hullabaloo, she heard Travis say, "I'll be waiting for you. Let me know when you're ready."

Her eyes snapped to his. Ready? For what? He nodded toward the tractor, its trailer already loaded with hay bales.

Lindy felt embarrassed heat tinge her cheeks. "You bet."

Travis turned and walked away, settling his broad shoulders against a tree several feet away. He aimed his gaze over her head, as if watching the horseshoe competition behind her, but he stayed within earshot.

Let me know when you're ready.

The low-lying sense of loss she'd carried all day swelled. Her throat clutched, but her emotions refused to be held down any longer. Hot tears pinpricked her eyes. She fluttered her lids closed, trying to wipe away the moisture.

No dice.

The overwhelmingly sweet scent of sugar assailed her nose as Tina lifted her grimy hand to Lindy's check, catching a fat drop on her finger.

"Lindy, why are you crying? You hurt?"

She looked into the worried little faces and saw their mother's warm brown eyes. Shame seeped into her, driving away the last of her self-pity.

"No, sweetie, I'm just a little sad, thinking about some of the people we love who aren't with us anymore."

"Like my momma?"

Lindy squeezed both arms around the little girl. "Yeah. And Pops."

Shelley worked her way into Lindy's embrace. "And your boy baby."

For an instant, shock stole Lindy's voice.

"Lindy doesn't have a boy baby," Tina said.

"Does, too. I heard Mrs. Beaumont talking about him."

Lindy was amazed at how easily these two young children discussed something ninety-five percent of the adults in this county wouldn't speak of in front of her.

Tina's little arms circled her neck. "Lindy, how come you didn't invite your boy baby to my birthday party? I wouldn't've minded. He probably wouldn't've eaten much cake."

"Oh, sweetie." She ducked her head into Tina's hair, returning the girl's hug. Her gaze sought Travis and found him, still within earshot, leaning against the tree, staring straight at her, deep sadness evident in his eyes.

She kept her chin buried in Tina's hair and her gaze locked to his. "My little boy died before he was born."

"How come he died? Was he bad?" Shelley asked.

Lindy forced her stare away from Travis and focused on the two sets of wide eyes before her. "Shelley, you know dying's not a punishment. Some people, like Pops, live a long time, then their bodies get too tired to keep living. And some people, like your momma, get sick, and the doctors can't make them better." Both little heads bobbed up and down in agreement. Sadly, death was not a new concept for these little girls.

She returned her attention to Travis, holding his stare hoping to make him understand. "Sometimes, accidents just happen. There's no reason for it. No one's to blame."

Lindy wiped another tear from her face before continuing. "While my baby was in my belly, we were in a car wreck. Since I was bigger and stronger, I only got hurt a little. But the baby got hurt bad enough that he had to go to heaven and become an angel."

From the corner of her eye, she saw Travis's body go rigid with the blame she knew he'd carried for a year. She desperately wanted to help him accept the fact that the accident, and the miscarriage, were not his fault.

"Did you cry?" Shelley whispered, adding her hand to the stack on Lindy's belly.

"Yeah, sweetie. I cried a lot."

"Did Mr. Lindy cry?" Tina asked.

"Yep, he did. And Travis was extra sad, because he thought he should've been able to protect our baby." Lindy fought the urge to look Travis's way again.

"Daddy still gets sad sometimes about not having Momma around," Shelley confided. "But he says big boys don't cry."

"I think big boys would feel better if they did cry. Crying makes the sadness go away some, doesn't it?"

"Yeah."

"So does remembering. It's like bringing them back for a few minutes," she said, feeling grateful to her lost loved ones who had surely guided her through this difficult conversation

Tina suddenly jumped up from Lindy's lap and clapped her hands. "So my momma and your boy baby and Pops all got to come to my birthday party!"

"Well, I guess they did. That makes it an even more special day." As the two girls raced off to rejoin the festivities, Lindy gave in to temptation and turned to face Travis.

He stood away from the tree in a circle of dappled sunlight, his arms locked across his chest, the inner hand clutched over his heart. Tears shone in his green-gold eyes.

Around them, the partygoers faded. Lindy felt cocooned in a world of forgiveness and healing. For the first time all day, she wasn't fighting to control her tear ducts. Her eyes remained dry. No more tears today.

Filled with a happiness she wouldn't have believed possible just thirty minutes ago, Lindy released the final remnants of her grief and winked at Travis, letting her lips curl into a genuine smile.

Travis's heart rate kicked into high gear as he watched the smile spread across Lindy's face. Relief surged through his system, cleansing him, washing away the veil of guilt that had been smothering him for nearly a year.

Sometimes, accidents just happen. There's no reason for it. No one's to blame.

Lindy may have been talking to the children, but Travis knew the words were meant for him. Forgiveness. She'd offered it to him and allowed him to forgive himself, as well.

Travis felt lightened. Happy. Hopeful.

For the first time since he'd received Chester Warfield's phone call, he felt he and Lindy could work things out. He dropped his arms and stepped forward, his focus riveted on Lindy. She'd finally cracked the door between them, and he didn't plan to waste the opportunity.

Before Travis could cover the short distance, a wall of denim sprung up between him and Lindy. Robertson, a gaggle of little girls at his heels, hauled Lindy off the ground, off her feet, and into his arms, spinning her around as the delighted group of future heartbreakers cheered him on.

"You ready for a hayride, ma'am?" Robertson's loud voice boomed.

Travis's steps stalled. Even from a distance, he could see Lindy's blush. From over Robertson's shoulder, Lindy's head shook slightly from side to side. Deep blue eyes beseeched Travis not to make a scene.

Her palms pushed against the broad chest flattened against her own. "Put me down, you big flirt." Her tone remained playful, but Travis recognized that lightbulb look in her eyes. She'd finally realized he was right about Farmboy's true feelings.

Travis swallowed the bitter taste of jealousy coating his tongue.

"As you wish, beautiful." Robertson slid Lindy's body down the length of his own.

Once her feet hit the ground, Lindy took a giant step backward. Lowering her voice to a more conversational level, Lindy said, "Danny, people are going to get the wrong impression about our relationship."

Robertson stepped forward, reclaiming the distance Lindy had just established, and ran his finger down her cheek, capturing a stray curl and tucking it behind her ear. "What's wrong with our friends and family knowing how much I appreciate what you've done for me and my girls today?"

Appreciation, my ass. Travis's fists clenched as his feet started moving again. *I told you once, Farmboy. Keep your hands off my wife.*

"Travis?" Alice Robertson's voice singsonged across the yard, stopping him in his tracks.

Struggling to bank his anger, he sucked in a calming breath and switched his attention from son to mother. Behind him, he heard Lindy calling the girls into the house for a pre-hayride trip to the bathroom.

"Come keep me company," Alice said, patting the lawn chair next to her in invitation.

Calling on every ounce of manners his mother had instilled in him, he nodded politely and sat, recalling the look in Lindy's eyes when she'd silently begged him not to cause a ruckus. He'd plot a better time and place to kick Farmboy's ass. Somewhere free of interfering women.

"I guess you're a newcomer to children's birthday parties?" The saccharine voice interrupted his revenge planning.

Forcing a polite smile, he faced the youthful grandmother who was fanning herself with a clean paper plate emblazoned with Barbie's portrait. She smiled at him with sympathy and humor. He got the feeling Alice knew exactly what kind of trouble she'd just curtailed.

"Yes, ma'am," he answered, glancing back to where Lindy was cycling the young girls through the house. "And I don't know whether to be fascinated or frightened."

"Best bet is a little of both." The twinkle in her eyes told Travis she knew he meant about more than just the party.

"I'll keep that in mind."

"I sure was glad you added that bit about Lindy's driving lessons to y'all's list," she said, switching topics with the ease of an experienced gossip.

Travis felt his neck flush. "You've seen the Ground Rules."

"Of course I have."

Travis shifted uncomfortably in the rickety lawn chair. "Well, I'm not sure it was such a good idea after all. The first time I put her behind the wheel, she freaked out and ran."

Mrs. Robertson snickered, sounding just like her grand-daughters. "Oh, my. I bet running scared like that really pissed her off."

Travis nodded in agreement. "I'm worried her pride will keep her from trying again."

Her fan stilled as she gazed at him steadily. "Don't you give up on her. She's every bit as stubborn as that grandfather of hers was, God rest his soul, but she's worth the effort."

Travis didn't respond. He knew it wasn't necessary.

"That's one of the reasons I'm glad to know you're here for her, young man." She patted his knee, as if praising a child. "I know that girl hates to admit it, but she needs someone to take care of her from time to time. We all do. It's human nature. That's why God designed us in pairs. You two belong together."

"Mrs. Robertson—"

She lifted her hand from his knee and fluttered it between them, as if she could wave away his objections. "I know it's none of my business what goes on between a man and a woman, but I've got eyes. I also see my son's feelings for Lindy."

"It's hard not to notice the way he looks at her."

"It's hard not to notice the way *you* look at her."

"She *is* my wife, Mrs. Robertson."

"Good point. Very good point. Have you mentioned that to her lately?" Her expression turned smug.

What did she expect him to do? March on over, throw Lindy over his shoulder like some caveman and force her to choose?

A chorus of giggles and cheers filled the late-afternoon air as the last of the little girls streamed from the house, headed for the tractor at a full run.

"Guess that's my cue." Grateful to escape this woman who saw way too much, Travis stood and headed for the crowd. He'd taken only two steps before her voice stopped him again.

"I also know, deep down, Lindy doesn't return my son's feelings. If she did, they'd still be together."

Turning slowly, Travis faced the older woman. He'd sensed something between Lindy and Danny all along, but confronting the facts sent pain pulsing through him. He fought for calm as visions of Lindy's birth control pills filled his memory.

"Didn't know about that, huh?" She folded her arms across her belly. "Yep, my Danny and Lindy dated for a whole year. Then he wised up and took notice of Barbara. Smartest thing he ever did. Never lost sight of that girl, either, until God took her away from us too soon. Problem is, when he started looking again, all he saw was Lindy. My boy's too hung up on the past to see the now."

"Why are you telling me this, Mrs. Robertson? Seems to me you'd want your son to have what he wanted." Wary,

Travis mimicked her crossed arm posture and studied the older lady.

Was she setting him up? Travis wondered if Robertson would stoop low enough to enlist his mother's help. The way things were going, anything seemed possible.

"I do want Danny to be happy. What he wants is the right woman to love him for the rest of his life. But Lindy's not that woman." Tears thickened Alice's voice, leaving Travis with no doubt she spoke from her heart. At some point, Alice Robertson had become his ally.

"How can you be so sure she's not the right woman for him?"

"Because, boy, any fool can see she's your right woman."

As if on cue, Lindy called his name. "Come on, Travis. We're ready for you!"

I'm ready for you, too, he thought as he followed the sound of her voice, like an ancient mariner surrendering to a siren's call, traveling headlong into the unknown.

Chapter Eleven

What was taking him so long?

Lindy forced herself to stop pacing the porch. Straining to hear Travis's footsteps, she ran her palms over her hips, smoothing imaginary wrinkles from the denim skirt she'd chosen for church this morning.

She flicked her wrist and checked the time. The grits still had twenty minutes to simmer. Fighting the urge to pace again, she leaned against a post, hoping to give the illusion of casually enjoying the sunrise.

If Travis didn't show up soon, she'd lose her nerve.

Last night, long after the party guests had said their goodbyes, she'd lain awake, too emotionally stirred for immediate rest. As the clock ticked forward, bringing an end to the last day of the worst year of her life, she faced facts.

As furious as she'd been when Travis rejected her

advances, he'd made the right decision. If they had resumed a sexual relationship at that point, they would've cheated themselves out of the fragile friendship growing between them.

The creak of the barn door opening snapped Lindy from her reverie. Drawing in a deep breath, she pressed her right hand over the butterflies in her stomach and abandoned her pretext of studying the morning sky.

He rounded the barn's corner carrying on a conversation with Rufus. One look at him and her breath flew from her lungs, her stomach butterflies morphed into hummingbirds.

Barn muck covered his boots—when did he start wearing *cowboy* boots?—and streaked his faded jeans. He had an open flannel shirt thrown over a tight white undershirt. An Atlanta Braves ball cap rode low on his head.

Lindy sighed. She couldn't help herself. He looked like he belonged here, in her world. In fact, if she didn't know better, she'd swear this was the only world he'd ever known.

Suddenly he ended his conversation with Rufus and looked directly at her, as if he'd been aware of her perusal the entire time. Beneath the cap's brim, his left eye closed slowly in a "gotcha" wink as a devastating grin curled his lips.

Struggling to appear unaffected despite the heat burning her cheeks, Lindy answered with a smile. "Good morning."

He bounded up the porch steps, Rufus at his heels. "You sure look purty this morning." Lord help her, he even *spoke* like he'd lived here all his life.

"Thanks. I'm, uh, having breakfast before I leave for church and wondered if you'd care to join me."

"For breakfast or church?" Travis asked, bracing one palm against the house and using the bootjack to remove his boots.

"Either. Both."

"Both sounds good. Give me fifteen minutes to shower and change."

"Okay. Oh, and, Travis? Church service is pretty casual around here. Most of the men just wear jeans."

"Are you worried about me overdressing again?"

"Well, if you start yanking your clothes off at church, the Ladies Auxiliary might have a group stroke."

"In that case, I'll wait till we get back home." His smile grew even brighter.

Lindy wasn't sure which idea caused her heart to race faster. Travis yanking off his clothes or hearing him call the farm home.

"Seriously, sweetheart, I'll behave. I promise." He crossed his heart and jogged inside, taking the steps two at a time.

Lindy followed him, moving at a much slower pace, and returned to the kitchen to put the finishing touches on the huge breakfast she'd prepared—bacon, scrambled eggs, cheese grits. Contrary to popular belief, this cholesterol fest was not an everyday thing. She'd just wanted to do something nice for Travis.

A few minutes later, Travis's footsteps echoed down the stairs as she pulled the homemade biscuits from the oven. When he entered the room, she pulled a jar of homemade fig preserves from the fridge and peeked at him over her shoulder. He wore a crisp white button-down shirt, the sleeves rolled up to expose tanned, muscular forearms. Black jeans showcased the length of his legs, and good golly, another pair of cowboy boots. She'd bet forty acres they were genuine ostrich skin.

The phone clipped to his belt ruined his whole look. "Do you have to wear that phone to church?"

His brow crinkled. "Guess not." The clip made a popping noise as he pulled it from his belt. "I've already spoken to Marge and my father this morning. I'm sure they can handle anything that comes up over the next hour or so."

God forbid his father should have to handle anything on his own. Travis placed the phone on the counter. Lindy considered "accidentally" knocking it into the sink and turning on the garbage disposal.

"Remember when you used to cook breakfast for dinner?" Travis snuck an arm around her and swiped a slice of bacon.

Lindy swatted his hand and snatched the bacon plate off the counter. "I had to make it at dinnertime. You never stuck around long enough in the mornings for breakfast," she reminded him, carrying the jam and the bacon to the table.

He transferred the last biscuit to the bread warmer and turned to face her. The heat in his eyes dried all the moisture from her mouth. "Correction. We never got out of bed early enough."

The backs of her thighs connected with the hard table. Heat warmed her cheeks again. "You promised you'd behave."

"I sure did, and I always keep my promises." He put the bread warmer in the center of the table and pulled her chair out. As she sat, he pushed in her chair then took his own seat.

Her foolish heart fluttered again. So what if the man had good manners? Racking her brain for a safe subject, Lindy's gaze landed on a mostly deflated birthday balloon dancing solo in the corner.

"I'm sorry if things were a bit awkward between you and Danny yesterday." She forced herself to meet Travis's stare. "He means well, but sometimes he gets carried away with his overprotectiveness."

Travis's eyes narrowed; his smile disappeared. "Like I said before, his feelings run deeper than that."

"At first, I thought you were crazy. I can't picture Danny and myself that way." She shrugged. "Now, I realize you're right, but I don't know what to do about it."

"You have to be honest with him. Denying his feelings and hoping they go away is a big mistake. In the long run, he'll be more hurt."

"He's already been hurt enough. They all have. I don't want to do anything to add to their pain."

"Then you need to talk to him."

Lindy nodded. "I know."

Danny was her oldest friend. Along with Barb, they'd been like the Three Musketeers—or more likely, the Three Stooges—since kindergarten. The last thing she ever wanted to do was break his heart. She'd have to pick her words and her timing very carefully, but Travis was right. She and Danny needed to talk. And soon.

But not today. She had different plans for today.

Travis drained his milk and set the empty glass down with a clatter that sounded overly loud in the quiet kitchen. "How about taking a ride this afternoon?"

The idea sent a ripple of fear down her spine. She wrinkled her nose, and asked, "How about tomorrow?"

That doubtful eyebrow of his shot up. "Procrastinating?"

"No, I promise. We can try again tomorrow afternoon, but I had something else in mind for after church."

"Good enough." He nodded. Lindy's heart warmed, knowing he trusted her to keep her word.

"So then, what's on the agenda?"

"Feel like exercising your brain instead of your brawn?"

"Lady, your wish is my command."

"Lindy, you've got to be kidding." Travis squinted against the afternoon sun, shaking his head in bewilderment.

"You said my wish was your command."

"Yeah, but I didn't think you'd wish for the impossible." He tossed the grayed board back onto the heap of scrap pieces lying next to the upside-down V-shaped roof truss.

"It's not impossible. Just difficult."

"Look, it's a great idea, but if you're going to build a pavilion, at least improve the odds by using new lumber."

"I can't afford new lumber."

"I'll buy it for you."

"No. Don't forget rule four. I don't want your money. Besides, the old wood will look more rustic."

"Rustic? Try dilapidated."

"Oh, come on. Use your imagination." She batted his shoulder before waving her arm over the scrap pile. "If we use this old wood, the cover will make the picnic area look like a natural extension of the setting. If you go out and buy new, treated lumber, it'll stick out like a sore thumb."

Travis eyed the aged wood. She had a point. The partial roof she'd recycled from an old barn *would* give the cover over the picnic tables a more germane look, but it would take twice as long to build. They'd have to clean-cut each plank and remove the rusty nails. Not to mention it'd be like assembling a giant jigsaw puzzle, trying to find boards with edges that lined up smoothly.

Travis looked at a smiling Lindy and knew he was a goner. If she wanted the damn thing built out of toothpicks, he'd find a way to make it happen. Anything to keep that beautiful smile on her face.

"Okay," he surrendered. "Let's do it."

Lindy threw her arms around him. Taken by surprise, he couldn't get his arms up quickly enough to return her hug before she stepped back, that radiant smile still lighting her face. "Oh, thanks, Travis. It's going to be great, you'll see."

Two hours later, they'd hammered out the details and drawn up a rough sketch of the finished project. Travis had to agree with Lindy's earlier assessment. If they could turn what was on paper into reality, the pavilion *would* be great.

Sitting next to him beneath the shade of a giant maple, Lindy once again focused on the picnic area. "I'll call Lester at the lumberyard first thing in the morning. Hopefully he'll have the posts and bags of sack crete delivered by the time we finish the morning chores."

Travis smiled at the enthusiasm in her voice. "Might as well get started digging those postholes today. That way, we should be able to get the posts set tomorrow and start putting on the supports Tuesday. Could be finished as early as Friday."

She lowered her hand and looked him in the face for the first time since surprising them both with her spontaneous hug. "Tomorrow will be soon enough to get started. After our mental workout, I think we deserve an afternoon off."

He flopped the pencil atop the yellow legal pad—the same one Lindy'd used for the Ground Rules—and stretched his legs out in front of him. "I gotta say, you missed your calling. With your ability to visualize not only the finished product but also the best way to make it happen, you should've been a construction foreman."

"Like you?"

"I was never really a foreman. I was just the boss's son, so the other guys had to listen to me."

"You may have been the boss's son, but that's not why your men paid attention to you. They respected you. I could see it, that first day we met, when you came in for lunch. You were just as sweaty and dirty as the rest of the guys, but there was something different about you."

"Good different or bad different?"

"Good different."

"You're blushing."

"I blushed then, too. Let's ignore it, like way back when."

"But you look so cute." Travis chuckled.

"Don't laugh at me or I'll change my mind about giving you the rest of the day off."

He locked his laughter inside, but could do nothing about the stupid grin he had plastered across his face. He hadn't felt this happy in a long time. "Yes, boss lady."

"Much better." Despite the stern tone, her lips twitched. "Do you really think we can get it all done so quickly?"

"I don't see why not, as long as the weather holds."

"That's fantastic. I'm hosting an open house for teachers and school administrators in a few weeks. It's really important that we look like a professional organization by then."

Travis caught the *we* and took heart. Whether she knew it or not, Lindy had begun to consider them a team.

"Don't worry, you'll wow 'em. You love what you do and it shows. I envy you that."

She propped her chin in her palm and turned curious eyes on him. "Why? No one loves their job as much as you do."

"I love the work. That's not always the same thing as loving the job."

"Even so, I'll bet you still miss it. Monroe Enterprises, the fancy office, the wheeling and dealing."

"Yes and no. I don't miss the company politics, but I do miss taking something most people see as useless and re-vitalizing it into something useful."

"Like turning old barn wood into a rustic—not dilapi-dated—pavilion?"

He returned her grin. "Yeah, like that."

"What about big-city life? Do you miss that?"

"I thought I did, at first. Then I realized I was just con-ditioned to the noise, the constant motion."

"So living in the country for the summer's not so bad, huh?" The blush on her cheeks, the spike in her voice, gave her away. This little inquisition had nothing to do with whether or not he missed fast-paced city life and everything to do with how he felt about the woman in front of him.

"It's great. Tennessee's natural beauty and peace and quiet are beginning to grow on me. Forces me to slow down and really think about the future, you know?"

"Yeah, but too much thinking's not always a good thing." She turned her face away, toward the pond.

"Why not?"

"Pops used to say you could think an idea to death. It's doing that makes things happen, not sitting and thinking."

"But action without thought can be a dangerous thing."

Lindy tapped the drawing in her hand. "That's why when it's really important, you balance the thinking and the acting, and when you're done, you've got something to be proud of."

Later that night, Lindy offered her reflection a nervous smile of encouragement. The girl in the mirror, wearing a hot-pink nightshirt with the slogan Coffee, Tea or ME! scrawled across her breasts, groaned in response.

"I can't believe *this* is the sexiest thing I own!" She yanked the shirt over her head and tossed it on the bed. Somewhere between yesterday's wrenching emotions and this afternoon's comfortable teasing, she'd stopped fighting her desire for Travis. Even though she knew it wouldn't change their basic differences, knew they still had no future, she wanted them to be lovers again.

Naked, she crossed to her closet, hoping to find something more suited to a seduction. Did it really matter what she wore? Travis had made his desire for her abundantly clear. He'd prefer she admit her feelings first, but judging by the looks he'd given her over breakfast, she could probably work around that.

Funny thing was, she didn't want to. She had a bucket-load of feelings for Travis. What would it hurt to admit she cared for him? That she considered him a friend?

Inside the closet, her fingers grazed a hanger covered with soft material. She pulled it out, surprised to find one of Travis's fancy dress shirts in her closet.

Holding the shirt against her bare skin, she knew there was only one explanation for this laundry snafu. "Alice, you old matchmaker."

Instantly deciding to forgive her buttinsky housekeeper, Lindy withdrew the hanger and slid her arms inside the shirt. The silky material carried a hint of Travis's scent and felt decadent against her skin. Buttoning up as she returned to the dresser mirror, she once again smiled at her reflection. This time her lips curled up in a sultry grin.

"Oh, yeah. This works."

Travis's shirt hung nearly to her knees and she left the top three buttons undone, showing just a hint of décolleté. Her grin widened into a full smile. Even her vocabulary sounded sexier.

She freed her hair from the collar and scrunched it. Her curls danced around her head. Desire shone from her eyes and the lipstick she'd applied earlier made her lips look fuller.

"The man doesn't stand a chance."

Turning toward the door, she rubbed a palm across her tummy, expecting nerves but finding excitement instead. Her blood seemed to hum, carrying liquid warmth throughout her body. Her skin tingled at the memory of his touch, of the way they'd fit perfectly together.

She stepped into the hallway, the hardwood floor cool against her naked feet.

Tiptoeing to Travis's door, she lifted a lapel to her nose, breathing in a dose of his unique scent. Yes, she could admit she had feelings for this man, join her body with his, enjoy the ecstasy only he could bring her. But her deepest feelings, those fluttering emotions entrenched in her heart? Those she'd keep to herself.

Lindy turned the cool metal knob and pushed the door open. The bedside lamp cast a dome of light, spotlighting Travis. He sat, pushed up against the headboard, his firm chest a tanned contrast to the white sheet riding low on his hips.

His head rested on the wall above the bed, his dark hair hanging nearly to his shoulders. He'd been staring out the window, but when she entered, his head swiveled in her direction. She paused in the open doorway, allowing his eyes to sweep over her.

"Am I dreaming?" His voice sounded the way scotch felt flowing down your throat. Rough and smooth at the same time.

She smiled and strolled leisurely to the bedside. "No."

"Thank God." His eyes made the trip to her feet and back again. "Every night I dream of you coming back, but this is the first time you've worn one of my shirts."

She held her arms out at her sides and felt the shirt's hem rise on her thighs. "Like it?"

"Love it." He closed his eyes for a second, as if relishing a vision. When his lids lifted, his eyes glowed more golden than green. "Does this mean what I think it means?"

She completed her trip across the room and lowered her body to the bed. "It means I want to continue the conversation we started last time I was here."

"That didn't end very well."

"Let's not think of the other night as an ending. Just a chance to retreat and rethink. Maybe our discussion's supposed to end tonight."

His eyebrows rose. "Where do you want to pick it up?"

"How about where you said if I'd admit I have feelings for you, you'd spend the next twenty-four hours making love to me?"

Travis sat forward, closing the distance between them. "Are you sure I'm not dreaming?"

"Touch me, Travis. I'm real."

From beneath the sheet, he lifted his hand and ran the back of his knuckles across her cheek, then opened his palm and cupped her face. "You're very real. Can I kiss you now?"

"Don't you want to hear about my feelings first?"

He drew in a deep breath then took his hand from her face and began twirling a blond curl around his finger. "Sweetheart, as much as I want this to mean more than just sex, I'm not sure it makes a difference anymore. I need you so bad, I'm willing to take whatever you offer."

She grabbed the hand playing in her hair and raised it to her lips, kissing each knuckle in turn before lowering his hand to the mattress, holding it between both of hers. "Travis, we've made a lot of mistakes in our relationship, but lately, I feel like we're beginning to get a few things right. We've become friends, something we never really did before."

"Guess we were too busy making love to become friends. This time, we did it in the right order."

"Yep." She squeezed the hand she held between hers. "This morning, I realized I was ready to move forward with my life, but until Pops's will is settled, we're both stuck in the here and now. We can't change the past and the future's on hold. This summer's like our moment out of time. So let's enjoy it." Lindy leaned forward, touching her lips to his.

Travis's free hand cupped the back of her head, holding her mouth against his for several long seconds. When he broke the kiss, he didn't release her head. "So, you're offering four months of no-strings sex and friendship?"

"Well, I was thinking the friendship might last beyond the summer, but, yeah, basically that's my offer."

Travis pulled her lips back to his. His kiss seared her like a tattoo. "I can accept that. For now."

"Thank goodness," she whispered against his mouth before shimmying forward on the mattress, bringing her silk-covered chest into contact with his.

"I want you to keep this shirt, sweetheart. It looks a helluva lot sexier on you than it ever could on me."

She ran her hands lightly through the hair dusting his muscled chest. "I don't know. I think this is quite a sexy look you've got going here."

With his hand still cupped against the back of her head, Travis rolled her onto her back, reclining her sideways across the bed, his lips sliding over hers. She yearned for his fierce possession. His touch remained gentle, almost reverent.

She opened her mouth beneath his, hoping to tempt his tongue into an erotic dance with hers, but he pulled back, peppering her neck with nipping kisses.

The moist warmth of his tongue burned her collarbone as Travis blazed a trail of kisses between her breasts. His hair, longer than she remembered, tickled her, drawing a moan from deep within her core.

"Travis—"

His lips curled into a smile against her skin. She'd never been so hot. He lifted onto his elbows and slipped her first button free, exposing the rise and fall of her breasts.

"I want to go slowly, but I need you too badly."

She thrust her hips forward and wrapped her legs around him. "You promised me twenty-four hours. Slow can wait till next time."

His fingers made quick work of the remaining buttons, laying the fabric aside, exposing her bare flesh to his heated gaze. He rolled onto his side, running a trembling hand over her stomach. "You're more beautiful than I remembered."

The sounds of their breathing filled the room as they stroked and stoked each other, the tempo building until Lindy clenched her thighs against his hand and cried out, spasms of pleasure gripping her body.

Travis's lips teased across her nipples, heightening her already overloaded senses. He swirled his tongue in the crevasse between her breasts as the first wave of shudders ran their course.

When her body stilled, she opened her eyes and found him studying her. She'd have purred if she could. "I lied earlier."

Beside her, Travis's body went rigid.

"I'd like to go back to your comment about burying yourself so deeply inside me, we'll forget we're two different people."

A wicked grin spread across his face. "Your wish is my command, sweetheart."

Travis rolled back over her, and with one swift thrust, joined their bodies into one. Beneath her fingers, his back muscles went taut. He held himself still for a second, waiting as her body stretched to accommodate his thickness.

His hands framed her face, his eyes boring into hers. "This changes *everything*."

Her hips surged against his, drawing him even more deeply inside of her. "Yesss!"

Their bodies rocked together in a well-remembered rhythm, picking up where their dance had left off a year ago without missing a beat. With each movement, the tension built deep inside her, pushing her to the edge of a sensual precipice she wanted to cling to forever.

Travis melded his lips to hers and with a final, powerful thrust, propelled them both off the edge and into the bliss. Lindy's body shook with the release that slowly and fiercely rippled through her system, starting in her center and radiating all the way to her heart.

Chapter Twelve

Travis snuggled deeper into the enticing warmth, hugging his pillow, clinging to the most intensely erotic dream of his life. His pillow attempted to pull free from his hold, so he tightened his grip and rubbed his cheek against the softness.

Then the husky Southern twang that had haunted his dreams for far too long spoke. "Chores."

The word did not fit the sexy images playing in his brain.

The pillow pushed against his chest. "Travis, turn me loose," Lindy whispered from somewhere below his chin.

Ah, man. Those weren't dreams playing in his mind. They were memories. Honest-to-God memories of all the wonderful, wicked things they'd done to each other last night.

He tugged Lindy, not his pillow, back against his chest and nuzzled his chin in her hair. "No. I promised you twenty-four hours and I plan to deliver."

Her breath fluttered across his chest as she chuckled. "You delivered plenty in the past eight hours."

Unadulterated masculine pride surged through Travis. He smiled, remembering. Four times. The memories awakened his lower half. Travis pressed his hips against her, showing her how she affected him. "Last night was just the beginning. I still owe you sixteen hours."

She put her hand on his chest and raised her shoulders off the bed. He opened his eyes, squinting against the glow of the lamp they'd left burning all night. Her hair cascaded around her face and the sheet slipped to her waist, exposing her breasts, revealing a patch of beard burn above her areola.

He scowled, tracing his fingers over the damage he'd done to her tender flesh. "Did I hurt you?"

Lindy pushed to a sitting position and flattened her hand over his. "No." Tender fingers smoothed the lines between his brows, tipping his head back until their eyes met. "I loved every second, every touch, every kiss."

His pride, among other things, surged again. Taking her by surprise, his arms snaked out and pulled her across his chest. "We never did get around to taking it slowly."

She braced her palms against his chest and tossed her hair out of her eyes. The movement ricocheted through her, grinding her nakedness against his. Travis's body twitched in response. He doubted he'd be any more able to deliver slow this morning than he'd been last night.

"Mmm." Lindy sucked her bottom lip under her teeth. "I'm looking forward to that slow thing, but right now, I've got to hustle. Thelma and Louise are not at all impressed with slow." She pressed harder against his chest and rose, throwing one leg over his body, obviously intent on leaving the bed.

His hands snatched her again, digging into the lush flesh across her hips, and settled her intimately across his lap. "How 'bout we make those two gals wait another thirty minutes? Just this once?"

Lindy wrinkled her nose and shook her head. Travis winced, keeping his eyes closed an extra-long second as he struggled with his disappointment. He certainly knew all about putting job responsibilities before personal desires, but, damn, he couldn't get enough of her.

"But I will make you a deal." The raw sensuality in her voice popped his eyes wide-open. Her irises were smoke rings around full black pupils Travis thought for sure he'd drown in.

"If you help with the milking, I'll give you fifteen minutes."

Travis didn't even have time to accept before she slid forward, encasing his arousal in her warm, moist center. Her laughter filled the room as she gripped the headboard and began to rock, back and forth, up and down, retreating until he nearly slipped free, then advancing with excruciating slowness, claiming his entire length. Her gaze held his, allowing him to see the immense pleasure she gained from setting the pace.

Then her laughter stilled and the look in her eyes shifted. Power replaced the pleasure. She thrust forward, slamming their bodies together. Her hips pistoned against his at supersonic speed. She removed one hand from the headboard and drew it behind her back. The smile on her lips turned downright sinful mere seconds before she cupped him.

Her touch wasn't timid or gentle and it nearly did him in. Oh my, if she didn't slow down—

Lindy stilled, her hips pushed as far forward as his body would allow, her inner muscles clutching him. From deep in her throat, she started making little purring noises.

He filled his hands with her hips once more, holding her steady as he thrust himself deep inside her. His release shot through him in a white-hot rush, the pleasure so intense he feared he'd pass out.

Lindy's head dropped to his shoulder, her lips trailing kisses along his damp neck. For several long minutes, neither of them moved. She lay on top of him, heart to heart, his body still wrapped tightly inside hers, until their breathing returned to normal.

His hand trailed down her back, over the curve of her rear and back up again. Forget twenty-four hours. Travis wanted to spend the next fifty years, right here, wrapped up in this woman. He didn't want to have sex. He wanted to make love. He wanted to make another baby.

His hand stilled. Whoa! Where'd that come from?

Lindy had fought their attraction for over a month before finally giving in, and then only after convincing herself this was a short-term affair. If he mentioned a possible future between them, let alone a baby, she wouldn't even speak to him for the rest of the summer much less sleep with him again. Ever.

Besides, if the birth control pills he'd discovered in the bathroom drawer were any indication, children weren't in her immediate plans.

Lindy snuggled deeper against his chest, drawing him back from his bleak thoughts. Her eyelashes tickled his skin. "Goodness gracious. That was—" she paused, kissing the underside of his chin "—incredible."

He squeezed both arms around her, holding her even more tightly. "Pretty damn intense, all right. You might need to take an extra one of those little green pills today, sweetheart."

The minute the words were out, Travis wished he could reel them back in. *Way to go, genius.*

Lindy tensed and pulled herself off him, all of him. Her face lost all color, and despite her clenched jaw, her chin trembled.

"Oh God, Lindy, I'm sorry. I'm an idiot."

She stood, pulling the sheet with her. This time, he lifted his weight, allowing the sheet to slip out from under him.

"I'm sorry you're an idiot, too." She turned her back on him, but not before he saw the glimmer of her tears. "Don't worry, Travis. The last thing on earth I want is to wind up accidentally pregnant with your child again."

"I don't want that, either."

She'd made it to the door, but his words, words that kept coming out terribly wrong, stopped her on the threshold.

Her shoulders tensed even more, something Travis would've thought impossible. "I'm glad we finally agree on something."

"No, that's not—"

The door closed behind her, leaving him lost and alone with his useless words.

"I want our next pregnancy to be intentional."

Despite the jagged crack running crossways through her heart, Lindy smiled as Lester Willard's flat-bed truck rolled down the driveway. Ten o'clock on the nose, exactly as promised.

Sighing, she turned away from the study window and retrieved the pavilion sketch and the list of supplies she'd ordered. She wondered, not for the first time, what kind of hold Travis had on her. From the tingly soreness between her thighs to the herd of butterflies in her stomach, she felt out of place in her own skin.

Last night had been so much more than she'd bargained for. For goodness' sake, this morning, his wicked smile had tempted her into delaying her chores. Then he'd made that horrible comment about getting her pregnant.

She'd held back tears all through the milking, and afterward, she'd returned to the house, grabbed a quick shower and sequestered herself in the study. She phoned Lester, paid a passel of bills and returned several long-overdue telephone calls. All legitimate business details, of course, but any pea-brain could see she'd been hiding.

Squaring her shoulders, she raised her chin and left the study. Time to get her head out of the sand. Yes, Travis's remark had hit a nerve, but he'd obviously been teasing. Frivolous pillow talk. That's what lovers did, right?

"Right." She knew Travis would never intentionally hurt her. As she headed for the door, her footsteps echoed in the empty hallway. Her answer echoed through her brain.

Right. Right. Right.

By the time she reached the front door, the word rang in her head with conviction, growing in importance, taking on a greater meaning.

Outside, she stepped off the porch just as Lester slammed the white cab door with Willard's Hardware and Lumber stenciled across it in bright red letters. He raised a silent hand in greeting. The delivery truck's passenger door slammed, echoing across the yard as Lindy returned Lester's wave, adding a big smile. Off to her left, footsteps approached from the barn. Her smile faded.

The papers she held crinkled in her tightening grip. She relaxed her fingers and waited in place, feeling suddenly shy, uncertain. What would she say to him? What would *he* say to *her?*

Last night, she'd made the first move. This morning, she would let him take the lead.

Travis stopped beside her, plunging the posthole digger he carried into the dirt and leaning against its long handle. His familiar scent of cedar and sea breeze mixed with the odors he'd picked up during morning chores. For some reason, on him, the smells combined in a way that stirred her heart.

They stood silently for a moment, staring toward the delivery truck, where Lester talked and gestured to a similarly attired fella.

"Sorry about sticking my foot in my mouth this morning." Travis's voice held that familiar self-deprecating tone she'd heard so much since his arrival in Tennessee. She loved that tone, loved that he didn't always take himself too seriously.

"I might have overreacted," she admitted, sneaking a peek from the corner of her eye. All she saw was his strong profile. "You took me by surprise, bringing up my birth control pills out of the blue like that. How did you know about them?"

"We share a bathroom, remember?"

Trying to pretend she *could* forget, she watched Lester and his helper offload a dozen cedar four-by-fours. "Oh yeah."

"Knowing you're on the Pill now, when you were so opposed before, has been driving me crazy."

"Why?"

"Makes me wonder why you changed your mind."

On the surface, it sounded like a simple question. But it was far from simple. After the miscarriage, she'd been an emotional wreck, terrified of becoming pregnant again, of risking the heartache of another miscarriage. Her doctor in Atlanta prescribed the pills, and she'd been taking them ever since.

She searched for the right words to explain, silently counting the bags of Redi-Mix stacked near the picnic area. Ten, eleven, twelve.

She breathed in deeply and offered the plain, ugly truth. "After the accident, I was afraid to risk another unplanned pregnancy. Now, I keep taking them for the convenience."

"Convenience? Not to avoid pregnancy?" His voice sounded rough, as if just asking the question caused him pain.

"Pregnancy hasn't been an issue until last night."

Travis's breath whooshed across her cheek. "The same goes for me, Lindy."

Shocked, she swiveled her gaze to him. "You mean, you haven't—"

He shook his head. "I'm still a married man," he whispered, raising a hand to stroke her cheek. "You've been the only woman in my life since the day we met, sweetheart."

"Oh, Travis." His name escaped in a husky sigh. She heard the posthole digger clang to the ground just as his hands gently gripped her shoulders, turning her to face him, bringing her dangerously close to his chest.

For once, she was unconcerned about the tears she knew shimmered in her eyes. His confession touched her soul, sparking tremors of trust she hadn't felt in a long time.

Right. Right. Right.

The papers she held became even more crumpled as she raised her hands to his shirtfront, holding him at bay. She craved physical contact, but she couldn't ignore their audience.

The heat in his eyes nearly melted her bones. Not to mention her resolve to keep their relationship under wraps.

"We're not alone." She flicked her eyes toward the picnic area where Lester was making some notations on a clipboard, probably tallying her invoice. In about sixty seconds, he'd be asking for her signature.

Travis muttered an obscene suggestion for dealing with Lester which Lindy chose to ignore. She lowered her hands. His arms continued to surround her so she raised one brow, the way she'd seen him do countless times. Travis growled deep in his throat. "This discussion is not over."

Taking a step backward, creating more of a buffer zone between them, she winked. "Oh, I'm counting on it."

Heat sparked in his eyes again, but thankfully, Lester's approach offered Lindy a valid distraction. Smoothing a not-quite-steady hand over her belly, she met Lester halfway.

"I can't tell you how much I appreciate your making this delivery on such short notice."

Lester tipped his hat without actually breaking the vacuum seal that thing had on his head. "No problem." His pale blue eyes looked over her shoulder to where Travis stood behind her. "I saw that old truss. Y'all have your work cut out for you, but once you get it done, that pavilion's gonna look right nice."

Lindy took the clipboard he extended toward her and quickly double-checked his figures before scrawling her name across the bottom. "I sure hope so. The picnic area's the last big project left before opening day."

"Mmm-hmm," Lester offered, tearing the yellow copy from the bottom of the clipboard and handing it back to her. His eyes took stock of Travis again, a head-to-toe perusal.

"Give Mavis my best," she said. "Tell her she and her new hip are in my prayers."

Lester gave another honorary tip of his cap, took one last look at Travis, nodded at Lindy then returned to his truck.

Travis closed the distance between them and draped an arm around her shoulders. Lindy stiffened her spine to keep from fusing herself against him.

"That was the quietest snoop I've ever seen," he chuckled, watching Lester's flat-bed truck rumble back down the driveway.

"It's a defense mechanism."

When Travis lifted his brows in question, Lindy laughed softly. "His wife would kill him if she found out he'd been out here and didn't have any news to report. Mavis is recovering from hip surgery, and Lester's her only source of new gossip. But once he reports, she'll spend the rest of her day on the phone, telling all her friends how worried she is about poor little old me, taking on too much."

"Everyone you know seems to feel justified in poking their nose into your business. Doesn't it ever bother you?"

"No. I'm used to it. They only worry because they care. Besides, I'm not the only one being discussed these days."

Travis snarled. "What do you mean?"

Laughing at his fierce expression, she threw her arm around his waist and continued her trek toward the picnic area. "Relax. No one in Land's Cross is going to spread nasty rumors about you. But I did overhear Edith Beaumont talking about how shaggy your hair's gotten since you moved here."

Travis bunched a handful of hair at his neck. "It is getting pretty long. Maybe I should run to town this afternoon, visit the local barber."

She pulled up short, directly beneath a large red maple. "Oh, but— Never mind."

"But what?"

"I think you look good with longer hair. It's sexy."

"Sexy, huh?"

"Don't go fishing, Travis." Embarrassment burned her cheeks. "You know perfectly well how good-looking you are."

"But what I want to know is, how good-looking do *you* think I am?" He trailed the backs of his knuckles down her cheek and under her chin, tipping her head back.

Lindy's eyes locked on to his mouth. Her tongue ventured out, wetting her lips as she whispered, "Very."

"Thank God," Travis groaned. Encircling both arms around her waist, he lifted her feet off the ground, bringing her lips to his in a ravaging kiss.

She wrapped her arms and legs around him and met his hungry lips full on. Her fingers slipped into the hair brushing his collar. "Very sexy," she said against his mouth.

She felt his fingers knead into the flesh at her hips, pulling her even closer, his desire for her pressing against her belly. Instinct forced her to tilt her pelvic bone, insinuating his arousal between her thighs.

A car horn blasted through Lindy's fog. Pulling back from the kiss, she looked over Travis's shoulder. Through the grove of trees shielding them from the driveway, she saw Shayna's dusty little compact park in front of the house.

Travis buried his face in her hair and muttered a string of curse words that summed up Lindy's feelings, as well. She pecked a kiss on his cheek then released her arms and legs.

Once her feet hit the ground, she held on a second or two more, waiting till her legs were steady. "Saved by the horn."

"Who says I wanted to be saved?"

"I know what you mean, but if Shayna caught us in full make-out mode, it wouldn't be long before the whole town knew about us."

"Knew what? That we're sleeping together?"

"Well, yeah. Can you imagine how hard that would be to explain?"

"What's to explain? We're married. Married people sleep together."

"But we're not your typical married couple. We'll only be together for a couple of months. I'd prefer we keep this relationship just between us."

"Why?" Travis's growl returned.

"It'll just be easier, that's all."

"Easier? For whom?"

"For everyone. I won't have to answer so many embarrassing questions after you're gone. And people won't start expecting the impossible."

"Meaning?"

"Land's Cross is a very old-fashioned community. If the townsfolk find out we're sleeping together, they're going to think we're reconciling."

"What's wrong with that?"

"Like I said last night, after the will's satisfied, we'll

both return to our own lives, so there *can't* be a reconciliation." Maybe if she said it often enough, she'd eventually sound more convincing. "But if folks get the idea in their heads, it'll make it more difficult for me to explain everything after the summer ends."

"I thought we weren't going to worry about the future for now." Travis's eyebrows lowered as he glared at her, drawing two deep grooves above his nose.

"Not worrying about it and sabotaging it are two entirely different things."

"Sabotage? Don't be so melodramatic." Travis raked a hand through his hair.

"I'm not being melodramatic. I know exactly what it'll be like after you're gone. The whispered questions, the endless parade of eligible grandsons and nephews designed to heal my broken heart."

"If it's all so horrible, why take the risk? Why start an affair with me at all?"

Because I can't resist you.

Because you have some incredible hold over me.

Lindy shook her head, sadly aware she couldn't admit those things aloud. Ever. If she did, she'd be handing Travis her heart again, and she'd promised herself she wouldn't do that.

"Because I can't get on with my life until I get you out of my system."

"What if you don't get me out of your system before the end of summer?"

The butterflies in her stomach finally calmed, leaving her feeling strangely lifeless. "It doesn't matter. Come September, we'll both have to start moving forward with our lives."

Chapter Thirteen

Later that afternoon, Lindy wiped the already clean vanity top and glanced sideways at the bathroom clock: 4:27. If she wanted to keep her word to Travis about a driving lesson today, she'd better get a move on.

"Come on, Lindy girl, you can handle this." She gave her freshly showered reflection an encouraging nod before heading downstairs to put the cleaning supplies away in the mudroom. "You're as ready as you'll ever be."

For the past week, she'd been sneaking outside after lights out to sit in Travis's car, hoping to increase her comfort level. The next logical step was another attempt at driving. Then the final phase: riding shotgun.

Her heart rate kicked into overdrive at the very thought of once again sitting in that vulnerable position.

"One step at a time," she reminded herself, borrowing

Travis's favorite phrase. Not allowing herself any more time to think, she headed upstairs.

About an hour ago, after they'd finished setting the support posts for the pavilion, Travis had come inside saying he needed to return several phone calls. His announcement had taken her by surprise, because he'd spent very few daylight hours working on company business during the past month. He honestly seemed to be distancing himself from Monroe Enterprises.

Amazing.

She paused outside Travis's door to tuck her blouse more securely into her shorts. Not stalling or primping, she assured herself, just pulling herself together.

Travis's muffled voice carried into the hallway. Trying to make her presence known without disturbing his phone conversation, Lindy knocked softly. The door, which had been slightly ajar, swung open beneath her gentle taps.

He sat behind his folding-table desk wearing a clean Georgia Tech T-shirt, his cell phone pressed to his ear. Dark hair fell across his forehead as he scrawled notes, apparently unaware she'd entered the room.

Now what? A subtle coughing fit? Back out and knock louder?

"Julia, you know good and well I can't come home until after Labor Day." Travis tossed his pen down and, lids closed, brought his fingers to the bridge of his nose, massaging the lines dissecting his eyebrows as he listened to whatever his former lover was saying into his ear.

A volatile mix of betrayal, rage and jealousy squeezed Lindy's heart until she could hardly breathe. Yesterday, he'd called the farm home, but today, with Julia, Atlanta was home.

The trust she'd felt this morning wavered. Old doubts crept back in. Was he chomping at the bit to return to his big-city life? Was he already making plans for his future? A future with Julia?

And why should she care? She'd established the rules for their affair. No strings attached, no future commitments.

But darn it, did he have to move on so quickly? Couldn't he be heartbroken for a week or two? Was that really so much to ask?

Be careful what you ask for, Lindy girl. You just might get it. Well, she felt like she'd gotten it with both barrels.

No longer in the mood to tackle her fear today, she started to back out of the open doorway.

"Hell, no." The cold anger in Travis's voice halted her escape. "I've already bailed his butt out once. He's got to learn to take responsibility for his own mistakes."

What? Lindy couldn't believe her ears. She had no doubt Travis was talking about Grant—who else's butt would he have bailed out?—only it sounded like he planned on letting Grant take the fall this time. That was even more amazing than Travis actually distancing himself from the company.

"He's not my problem anymore." Travis's fingers pressed against his forehead for a few seconds before he dropped his hand and opened his eyes. He noticed her immediately, his eyes widening as he quickly flopped his notepad over and jumped to his feet.

"I have to go. Either handle it yourself or ask for Marge's help." He slapped his phone shut with undue force, not bothering with a proper sign-off and shoved a stack of paperwork on top of the notepad he obviously didn't want her to see.

Did he honestly think she was interested in the notes he'd scrawled while talking to that woman? As if.

She raised her chin and looked him square in the face. No way she'd rail at him like a jealous shrew.

"Sorry to disturb your *work*." She stressed the last word, letting him know she didn't care one bit about his business, professional *or* personal. "I promised to try another driving lesson this afternoon, and the afternoon is almost gone."

Travis consulted his watch and cleared his throat. "No problem. That was my last call. I'm ready whenever you are."

Yeah, right.

"You seem a little flustered, Travis. Problems at the office?"

Travis cleared his throat again and focused in the vicinity of her collar. "No, the company's running smoothly. That was a family matter, but it's, uh, taken care of now."

Why was he feeding her half-truths? Did he think she'd go ballistic if she knew he was still in contact with Julia? Of course, for a second there, she'd wanted nothing more than to drop kick his butt and hog tie him with the phone cord, à la Dolly Parton in *Nine to Five,* but she'd resisted and the urge had passed. Well, mostly.

She poured an extra scoop of saccharine into her voice. "Glad to hear you have things at *home* under control."

"Yeah, uh, thanks." He clipped his phone back onto his belt and rounded his flimsy desk. "Why don't we go on outside and get started?"

"You bet." She pivoted on her heel and headed downstairs.

"I noticed you've been spending time in the car," Travis said as he followed her down the stairs.

She cast a quick glance over her shoulder as she reached

for the front doorknob. So much for her sneaking skills. "How'd you know?"

"Because it smells just like you."

By now they were outside, and she'd almost reached the car. As she always did, she stopped, drawing in a few cleansing breaths before moving any closer.

"Yeah, I've been coming out the past several nights and just sitting behind the wheel. Well, sort of behind it. I keep my feet on the ground, but I put my butt in the seat and that's got to count for something."

Travis stepped up behind her and put a hand on her shoulder. She shrugged off the contact.

"Don't be nervous. You can set the pace. I won't push. You can trust me."

How could she trust him when he hadn't been straight with her just a few minutes ago?

Lindy took a step closer to the car, a step farther from his tender words, and spun to face him. Last year, she'd stormed off without discussing Julia's impact on their relationship. She wouldn't make that mistake twice. "Can I, Travis? Can I really trust you?"

His brow wrinkled. "Of course."

She studied his face for a long moment, waiting for another flicker of guilt or deception. She found none.

"Who were you talking to when I came in a minute ago?"

"Why do I think you already know?"

"Just answer the question."

"Julia," he admitted.

"You thought you needed to hide that, and your notes, from me?"

His shoulders sagged, as if the weight of the world had

crash-landed there. "I wasn't trying to hide anything. I didn't want to upset you by mentioning her name."

"Why would I be upset by that? I've made it clear that our relationship is only for the summer. Whatever plans you make for your future are none of my business."

Hurt by her own words, she tried to turn back to the car, but he grabbed her arm, keeping them face-to-face. "You think I'm planning a future with *Julia?*"

When he said it out loud like that, with a heavy dose of incredulity, it sounded pretty ridiculous, even to Lindy's jealous ears. She shrugged. The lump in her throat made a response impossible.

"Lindy, sometimes you can be so thickheaded." The smile playing around his lips somehow turned the insult into an endearment. "The absolute last person I want to spend my future with is Julia Wellborne."

Relief shrunk the lump in her throat. She swallowed. "Really?"

"Really. For one thing, she's the most conniving woman I've ever met in my life."

She liked the sound of that.

"Not to mention," Travis continued, releasing his hold on her arm and raking his fingers through his hair, "she's currently got her claws in Grant, which serves her right. Grant's more trouble than a dozen Julias."

Lindy bit the inside of her cheek to keep from grinning.

"As far as my notes go, they had nothing to do with Julia or Monroe Enterprises. I've just started a new project. When I know for sure whether or not my plans will work out, I'll be proud to share my ideas with you."

"Really?" Oh, hell. She sounded like a stuck record.

"You know, this wasn't the first time I've accidentally over-heard a private conversation between you and Julia."

"What do you mean?"

She sighed. "My last night in Atlanta, I came down to the office to surprise you, but you weren't alone."

Travis's brow furrowed and Lindy could practically see him rewinding the tape of his life. "You were there that night?"

"Yep. And I heard the two of you talking about how much longer you'd have to wait before sending me 'back to the sticks.'" Even after all this time, the embarrassment of that moment flamed her cheeks. She turned away from him, but his hand gently touched her shoulder and kept her from storming off.

"Is that all you heard?"

"That was enough."

"If you'd listened another minute longer, you'd've heard me tell her I wasn't interested in shipping my wife off anywhere." Exerting the gentlest of pressure, he urged her to face him. "Sweetheart, I'd just discovered Julia was behind a takeover attempt against Monroe Enterprises. That was a big reason I was working so many hours following the accident, why I wasn't there when you needed me."

Travis's warm hand cupped her cheek, his thumb tucking under her chin and lifting her face. "Sorry I wasn't up-front with you, then and now. I didn't want to cause a rift between us, but I guess I did anyway." He skimmed his thumb across her lower lip. "Thanks for calling me on it."

Her heart burst with happiness. "Thanks for trusting me with the truth. About then and now."

"I do trust you, Lindy."

For several long seconds, they stood beside his car in the late-afternoon shadows. Lindy watched the starburst appear in the green depths of his eyes and knew he wanted her. The feeling was very mutual.

But first things first.

She breathed deeply, drawing her courage up from the bottoms of her feet. "How about a trip out to the mailbox?"

Lindy was amazed by Travis's patience. After she'd settled in the luxurious leather bucket seat, it had taken her nearly ten minutes to talk herself into drawing her feet inside the car. Another couple to force herself to shut the door. Engaging the engine had been a quick decision—she couldn't roll down the windows until she started the engine.

Through it all, Travis sat completely still and quiet. For over fifteen minutes, she squeezed the steering wheel beneath her sweaty grip and steadied her nerves. Finally, half an hour after opening the door, she grasped the gearshift and put the car into Drive.

Travis's warm hand settled on her shaky knee. She chanced a glance in his direction and met his reassuring smile. Her lips turned up in a wobbly response. He gave her leg a slight squeeze then returned his hand to the passenger side.

"Here we go," she whispered. She could hardly hear her own words over the *thump-thumping* of her heart.

She had the brake pressed to the floor under both feet. Moving her left foot aside, she lifted her right several inches, allowing the car to creep forward. The familiar crunch of gravel traveled through the open window, the same as it did when she white-knuckled her way to town in Pops's old truck.

"I can do this." She heard the confidence in her own voice and completely released the brake, switching her foot to the accelerator.

She kept her eyes glued forward, but her pulse had calmed enough for her to hear Travis's soft chuckle. "Of course you can do it, sweetheart. You're the most determined person I know."

"You mean stubborn."

"Yeah, sometimes, but the two often go hand in hand."

"Diplomatic as always."

"I meant it as a compliment. You're a very focused woman, Lindy. When you set your mind to something, you don't let anything get in your way. Not even yourself."

"Not always." She'd set her mind on creating a real marriage with Travis, but she'd turned chicken at the thought of competing against the sophisticated Julia, whom Travis *hated*.

Reaching the mailbox, she stopped the car and turned to face him. His smile radiated pride.

"Attagirl!" He swooped down for a quick kiss. "Now, what do you say I drive us back to the house?"

His grin assured her he was only teasing, but the challenge set off a low-grade panic nonetheless. The leather seams in the steering wheel bit into her palms as she tightened her grip. "What happened to one step at a time? Letting me set the pace?"

"So that's a 'no'?" He chuckled again, diffusing her uneasiness.

She took a deep breath and slacked her grip. "That's a 'not yet.'"

* * *

Late Friday afternoon, Travis watched from the front porch as Lindy made the round trip to the mailbox in less than ten minutes. When she returned, she jumped out and pumped a triumphant fist in the air before launching herself up the steps and into his waiting arms.

He held her tight, burying his face in her hair. This had been the best week of his life. Every day, he and Lindy worked side by side, building the pavilion over the picnic tables. They'd finished the job today, and he had to admit, she'd been right. The old wood made the structure look like a natural extension of the land.

And, after working together all day, they played together all night. He made love to his wife—they'd finally gotten around to doing it slow—then slept with her wrapped tight in his arms.

He'd never felt more centered, more complete. Not even when they'd been together before the accident. In those days, their relationship had been based almost solely on sexual chemistry. But now, they were friends and partners, as well as lovers.

Lindy squeezed him around the waist and started to pull away. He inhaled the sweet fragrance of her hair once more and, calling on every ounce of his resolve, dropped his arms and allowed her to step out of his embrace.

Looking down into her smiling face, he cursed himself a fool. He'd finally found what he'd been searching for all his adult life, but the woman he loved, the woman he wanted to spend the rest of his life with, was only in it for the sex.

"Man, what a day." Hips swaying, Lindy danced a victory jig across the porch.

Every muscle in Travis's body, especially those directly below his belt, tensed. Success made her even sexier.

He stuck his hands in his pockets to keep from throwing her over his shoulder and carrying her upstairs, locking her in the bedroom until she promised to give them a real second chance.

"I say this day calls for a celebration."

She stopped dancing—thank God—and turned her smiling face up at him. "What did you have in mind?"

A thousand suggestions leaped to mind, but Travis pushed them all to the back burner. Tonight, he intended to romance her into admitting she still had deep feelings for him. Otherwise, once the will was satisfied, she'd send him packing.

He couldn't let that happen. His time on the farm had proven to him that they belonged together. There had to be a way to make their relationship work.

"How about a picnic tonight under the new pavilion, then a moonlight drive? You, of course, get to drive." He lifted one brow before adding, "Unless you'd rather I drive."

Her smile faded just a bit but didn't disappear altogether. "How does a moonlight stroll around the pond sound instead?"

She was playing right into his plans. "Deal."

The newly completed pavilion provided the perfect ambience for a romantic picnic. Travis lit half a dozen citronella candles and carried out a portable stereo. Classical music accompanied the singing crickets. Lightning bugs flitted among the trees while a full moon floated overhead.

By some unspoken agreement, they'd both dressed for the evening. Deciding against his "city clothes," he'd changed into the same black jeans and white shirt he'd worn to church. Judging by the thorough once-over Lindy'd given him when she thought he wasn't looking, he guessed it was the right choice.

Dressed in a vibrant blue dress, Lindy looked good enough to eat. The color complemented her eyes, making them look as blue and fathomless as the ocean. Her full breasts moved freely beneath the scooped neck, and the cinched waist showed off just enough curve to drive a man crazy without appearing blatantly sexy. Of course, on Lindy, a flour sack would be blatantly sexy.

Alice, who'd misted up a bit when Travis asked for her help in arranging this romantic evening, had packed a picnic basket filled with fried chicken, potato salad and coleslaw. The little old matchmaker had even stuck in a bouquet of fresh flowers.

After they'd fed each other every delicious bite of dinner, he'd suggested they stroll around the pond before tackling the still-warm apple pie tucked into the bottom of the basket.

This far from the candles, the moon's glow provided the only illumination. Even in the semidarkness, when he leaned his face close to hers, he could detect a hazy glow in her eyes. He hoped that warmth came from more than the bottle of Chianti Alice had included in their celebratory picnic.

Clearing his throat, he turned his attention to the beauty of the night sky, hoping the distraction would allow him to retain a modicum of self-control.

"I love how dark it gets here. You can see every star in the sky."

Lindy tucked her hand into the crook of his elbow as they slowly negotiated the darkened path, heading back to the picnic area. "When I was a little girl, Pops and I used to lie out under the stars on clear nights like this. He'd point out the constellations and I'd dream of being a pioneer woman, navigating by the stars and taming the Wild West."

"Um, I bet you looked great in leather chaps."

"Darned tootin'. And they came in mighty handy since I refused to ride sidesaddle."

"So, you were stubborn even in your childhood fantasies."

"I thought you said I was determined."

"Yeah, but why split hairs?"

She nudged a gentle elbow into his ribs. He sidestepped the blow and captured both her hands, gently twisting them behind her and guiding her backward until his knuckles rasped against the trunk of a giant pine. Releasing her wrists, he propped his hands on either side of her face and stepped forward.

Using his knee, he nudged her legs apart as far as her skirt would allow and insinuated himself between them. Taking a page from her book, he pressed his hips forward, grazing his erection across her stomach.

Balancing her weight against the tree, she wrapped her bare right foot around his calf. He lowered his head, but rather than fitting his mouth over hers, he joined them forehead to forehead and drew in several ragged breaths.

She arched her back and threaded her fingers through his belt loops, drawing his chest tight against her breasts. "Kiss me, Travis."

He raised his head and let his index finger run the length of her cheek, headed for the lushness of her lips. At the last second, his touch detoured, trailing instead over her jaw, down the side of her neck. Continuing south, he outlined the dip of her collarbone, the curve of her shoulder. As he drew an invisible line down the silky smoothness of her arm, he felt her shudder, heard her breath escape in a sigh that sounded remarkably like his name.

Finally finding her hand, he disentangled her from his jeans and entwined her fingers with his. Lifting their joined hands, he caressed his lips over her knuckles.

She gyrated against him and he pressed his hips more snugly against hers, sandwiching her between him and the tree, stopping her movements. He needed to rein himself in. If he didn't get control of himself soon, he'd end up taking her right here, nailing her against a tree like some deranged animal. How romantic would that be?

"Travis." She sighed, the hand still twined in his belt loop tugging at him. "Kiss me, or I'll have to hurt you."

Travis claimed her second hand, once again dropping kisses across her knuckles. "Sweetheart, you should never threaten a man when he's gone to so much trouble to romance you."

He brushed his lips lightly against hers and heard another of her sexy sighs. He brushed her lips again, not so lightly this time, and felt a tremor pass through her. On his third pass, her mouth opened slightly, her tongue darted out, teasing his lips as they crossed hers.

"You taste so good," he whispered against her cheek. "I think I'll have you for dessert instead of apple pie."

"Oh, yes." Another tremor shook her body. "Travis, let go of my hands. I need to touch you."

"If you touch me, I'll never make it into the house."

"So? Make love to me here, under the stars." Her laugh floated on the night breeze along with the scent of jasmine.

He drizzled kisses along her collarbone, using his chin to nudge the dress aside. "Um, I love the way your mind works."

The whisper of her name floating from Travis's lips tickled Lindy's ears, vibrating through her, quivering her nerve ends as if he'd touched both sides of her skin, when in fact, he hadn't touched her at all.

Increasing her arm's pressure around his neck, she strained closer toward him, silently insisting he meld their bodies. She yearned for his weight, needed to feel the heaviness of his erection, to know that soon, very soon, he'd prick the bubble of desire building within her, sending that sweet rush of release throughout her system.

She parted her lips, and—yes!—he seized the moment, slipping his tongue inside her mouth. Changing her grip to his shoulders, she grasped a fistful of cotton in each hand and let her knees buckle, using her body weight to propel him closer.

His rock-solid chest touched her, pressing her back against the tree, flattening the flesh of her breasts while peaking her nipples. Their hips joined next, his muscles firm against her soft belly. It wasn't enough. She wanted more—fingers caressing, teeth nipping, lips sucking. She wanted it all.

Travis broke the kiss, shifting slightly to nuzzle her neck. His ragged breath warmed her skin as their chests heaved in unison. One hand trailed from her hair to cup her breast.

Finally.

She pressed herself more firmly against his palm. "Yes, please. Touch me, Travis. Everywhere."

His free hand quickly slipped into the space she'd created between her back and the tree. The rasp of her zipper filled her ears as he lifted his face to hers.

"I want to touch every glorious inch of you." His hands moved to her shoulders, caressing the skin beneath her loosened dress. His hands trembled slightly as he smoothed them down her arms, the blue material of her dress pooling around her waist. In anticipation of just this moment, she'd forgone a bra. Cool night air blew across her naked breasts, tightening her nipples even further. She felt the force of his gaze, as tangible as any caress.

"Beautiful," he whispered, wrapping his arms around her waist, lifting her, aligning her breasts with his lips. Dizzied, she closed her eyes and balanced her hands on his shoulders, bracing for the onslaught.

The world tilted on its axis, spinning Lindy with it. Something cool and damp tickled her naked back. Her eyes popped open, seeing a million stars haloed around Travis's head as he laid her in a patch of grass near the pond.

He is *romancing me.* Her heart wanted to soften, but she refused to let it. Their affair was supposed to be about sex. Just sex. He had no business making her *feel* so much.

Thankful that her hands were steady, she yanked his shirt free of his waistband and worked his buttons loose. "Off," she ordered, parting his unbuttoned shirt so she could slip her arms around him. She pulled him over her, settling him between her legs.

Their bodies were a perfect fit, hills and valleys nesting

into a new and better whole. His mouth took possession of hers once again. She could feel the tense restraint in the muscles bunched beneath her palms. His tenderness caused an unexpected rush of tears to sting her eyes.

He makes me feel too much, want too much.

Lindy transferred her hold to his belt, fumbling the leather through its buckle. She made quick work of his snap and zipper then steered her hands around his slim hips and dipped into his pants with both hands, cupping his tightly muscled cheeks and drawing him closer to her center. "Too slow. Faster."

"I thought this was fast."

"Not fast enough. I need you *now*." She tried to tug his jeans lower, but with his groin pressed so intimately against hers, those jeans weren't going anywhere.

She uttered an unladylike curse. A chuckle rumbled through Travis, causing his chest hairs to twitch against skin so sensitive she thought she'd explode with pleasure.

Before she could reissue her curse, another sound rumbled through the night air. They both froze, like teenagers caught making out in the backseat of the family wagon. Lindy cocked her head and listened as the rumble grew louder, competing with the sounds of their labored breaths and the crickets' song until she recognized its source.

A large truck, diesel judging by the noise level, crunched down the driveway located on the other side of the pine grove. Lindy pushed up onto her elbows and squinted through the trees. Sure enough, she saw a faint beam of light, growing brighter and closer with each second.

"Someone's coming," she stage-whispered.

Near the house, a car door slammed.

Travis retracted himself from the vee of her legs and rested back on his heels. "Sounds like they're already here."

A shiver raced through her, not from the cool night air against her fevered skin, but from a source as old as time. Female intuition. Whoever had just shown up after nine on a Friday night hadn't dropped by for a casual visit.

"*Liinnndeee!* Come out, come out, wherever you are!" a familiar deep voice singsonged across the barnyard.

Travis's brows rose. "What the hell is Robertson doing here?"

Lindy snagged the material bunched around her waist and tried to cover herself. "I have no idea."

The springs of the front screen door squeaked. Danny hollered her name a second time then began pounding on the door.

"Sounds like he's been drinking."

It certainly did. That couldn't be a good thing. "I should go see what he wants." She tried to put her arms back through her sleeves while keeping the dress pinned to her naked chest.

"Right now? Can't you just ignore him till he goes away?"

A loud "Oof" echoed across the yard, followed by the distinctive clunking of an overturned metal pail.

"I don't think so." Abandoning her attempts at keeping covered while dressing, she quickly untangled her bodice and shoved it back into place.

Travis pinched the bridge of his nose, muttering a vivid stream of curse words under his breath. When another loud clunking noise ricocheted across the still night, he lifted his head and took her hand.

"Damn it. Let's go see what Farmboy wants."

Chapter Fourteen

.

Travis fought the urge to howl as he watched Lindy's silhouette leave the romantic setting he'd created and rush toward the house. Danny had finally stopped screaming her name, but Travis wasn't sure the drunk man's rendition of Eric Clapton's "Wonderful Tonight" was an improvement.

Following at a slower pace, he kept Lindy in sight. He'd be running by her side if his zipper wasn't trying to peel away his most sensitive flesh with every step.

He drew in several deep breaths, searching for the calm control that used to rule his life, before Lindy had turned him inside out. The tightness in his pants eased and he readjusted himself and stepped out of the shadows.

The warbled singing ended when Robertson spotted Lindy.

"Liindeee!"

Travis heard her soft voice answer but couldn't discern her words over the distance separating them. Quickening, he drew near enough to see the big man on Lindy's porch clearly. Jeez, Robertson looked like he'd been on a three-day bender.

His stained and wrinkled shirt hung half out of his waistband. His eyes were bloodshot, and sand-colored stubble covered his chin. The porch light illuminated dried tear tracks running down his face.

Robertson tripped off the bottom step, stumbling toward Lindy, who braced her hands against his chest. She staggered backward a couple of steps before gaining purchase and propping Robertson back on his feet.

Travis sprinted toward them, tortured by visions of an injured Lindy crushed under the weight of a toppled Robertson.

"Nisch catch, beau'ful."

"Danny, what are you doing here like this?"

"Came ta shee my besh girl." He attempted to loop an arm around Lindy's shoulder, but his inebriated aim was off. His huge hand nearly smacked her cheek, but thankfully, Lindy tipped her head backward and avoided all contact.

Still, the threat of danger was enough to kick-start Travis's need to defend the woman he loved. He tackled Robertson, his momentum carrying them both to the ground.

Sobriety gave Travis the advantage. Straddling Robertson's chest, he quickly pinned the other man to the ground, a fistful of collar clutched in his left hand, his right clenched and cocked, ready to hammer a long-awaited blow to Farmboy's jaw.

Something silky and strong slipped over his raised fist.

He glanced over his shoulder at the unseen force attempting to waylay him. Lindy had a double grip on his hand. A kaleidoscope of emotions churned in her wide blue eyes.

"Travis, please don't." She kept her hands wrapped around his, lowering his fist as she sank to her knees.

He forcefully released the other man's shirt, dropping Robertson's head against the hard dirt. "He nearly hit you."

"Not on purpose."

"Is that supposed to make me feel better?" He uncurled his fingers and forced his shoulders to relax. As much as he wanted to punch Robertson, he wanted to earn Lindy's trust more.

"Thank you," she said gently. "I can handle him from here."

Did she honestly think he'd leave her alone with Robertson in his current condition? No telling what the idiot could do to her. He opened his mouth to argue, but Lindy halted his words with a warm fingertip against his lips.

"Danny's not likely to tell me what's wrong when you're scowling over him."

She was right about that, but still… "Fine, but I am not leaving you alone with him." He waited until Lindy nodded in agreement before shifting off Robertson.

Reluctantly, Travis stood. Walking backward, he covered the five steps to the front porch without taking his eyes off Robertson. As long as Farmboy remained conscious, Travis intended to keep Lindy within quick reach.

Robertson tried to rise from the dirt, but Lindy quickly assumed Travis's vacant spot, pressing her knee into Robertson's chest. The frown on her face and the angry set of her shoulders calmed Travis's fears. The lady was pissed.

Robertson was about to get it, and Travis had a front-row seat.

"You're acting like a real jackass tonight, Danny. Where are the girls?"

"Home."

"Who's watching them?"

"Shayna."

"Well, at least you had enough sense to make sure they were okay before you drank yourself into a stupor."

Robertson winced, Lindy's words apparently hitting home. Ignoring the man she had pinned to the ground, she glanced over at Travis. "I can't believe I'm asking this, but…" She drew in a deep breath. "Can I borrow your phone?"

For a moment, her words confused him. She'd made it obvious she hated his cell phone, hated the tie it represented to his family. And now she wanted to borrow it? Could this night get any more surreal?

"I don't have it on me."

She smiled shyly. "You don't?"

"You were the only person I wanted to talk to tonight."

Her smile grew.

"Got mine." Robertson's words drew Lindy's attention. She patted him down and pulled a flip phone from his front jeans pocket. Without a word, she dialed.

"Shayna? It's Lindy. Danny's over here and he's totally tanked."

As she listened to the other woman's answer, Travis could see her anger fade. She pulled her lower lip between her teeth and looked his way again. Tears glittered in her eyes.

"Oh Lord, I can't believe I forgot," she whispered.

"We'll make sure he gets home safe." She swiped away the tears hitting her cheeks.

Lindy closed the phone and let it fall to the dirt. She clutched Robertson's shirtfront and hauled him to a sitting position before wrapping her arms around him.

"Danny, I am so sorry. I forgot today was your anniversary." Her voice hitched.

A huge sob broke from deep in the big man's chest. His body trembled, his head lolled precariously for a second before Lindy steered it to her shoulder, tucking it under her chin.

Travis cringed, the animosity toward Danny he'd become comfortable with dissipating. He could understand some of the man's grief. He remembered his own wedding anniversary earlier this year, their first. And like Danny, Travis had spent the evening drinking himself stupid rather than making love to his wife.

Sooner than Travis expected, Lindy's tears dried up and she loosened her hug. "I can't believe the date slipped by me. Can you ever forgive me?"

"'Coursh I can, Lindy. I love you."

Travis stiffened. *I love you.* Those were the words he'd been dying to say to her for weeks now.

"That's what all this ruckus is about? Of course you love me. I love you, too. But I'm not *in* love with you any more than you're *in* love with me."

Danny opened his mouth to speak, but she cut him off. "You know, it would piss Barb off to know you were hiding behind your feelings for me instead of getting on with your life." The tenderness in her voice softened her harsh words. "Barb wouldn't want you to be alone for the rest of your life. She'd want you to find someone to love and grow old with, a woman who'd be a good mother to her children. But that can't be me."

She leaned in and placed a passionless kiss on his lips. "Don't waste any more time wallowing in the past, Danny, or you'll miss your chance at a happy future."

Travis hoped Lindy was listening to her own advice. She, too, clung to the mistakes they'd made in the past and branded their relationship impossible, refusing to acknowledge that they'd both changed. Grown.

Sure, when they'd flown off to Vegas, they may not have had what it took to make a marriage work. But they damn sure did now. If she'd let him, he planned to convince her that happiness waited around the corner for them, together.

But before they could face the future, the present needed to be cleaned up. He stopped beside Lindy and touched her shoulder. One of her hands automatically lifted, grasping his. Despite the mild evening temperature, her skin felt cold. He wanted to scoop her up and carry her inside, to offer her his strength and comfort.

"What can I do to help?" he asked. He couldn't bundle Lindy up and shield her from life's unpleasantness, but he could stand by her side and help her through the hard times.

"Would you mind running Danny home?"

"No problem." He'd volunteer to drive the man to Pluto if Lindy asked.

She turned her attention back to Danny. "Travis is going to take you home. Tomorrow, when you can see straight, take a good look around. You might be surprised to find you're closer to moving on than you think."

In one fluid move, Lindy bounced to her feet and held

her hand out to her friend. Danny slipped his enormous paw into her much smaller hand and allowed her to help him to his feet.

Travis followed a lumbering Robertson toward his truck. It took two tries, but Danny finally managed to open the passenger door. As soon as he pulled his size-sixteen boots into the cab, Travis slammed the door and rounded the hood. Lindy was holding the driver's door open, her face lit by the glow of the dome light.

He wanted to crush her against his chest, hold her there and never let her go. He wanted to tell her he loved her. That he was sorry he'd hurt her. That he didn't want to end up a few years down the road like Danny, trying to get on with his life without the woman he loved.

But the words would have to wait. As long as Lionel's will was responsible for his presence in Tennessee, Lindy would never trust his feelings. But the second Lindy took legal possession of the farm, when he could stay in Land's Cross by choice, nothing would stop him from telling her how he felt.

He had no idea how she'd react. Would she cling to her belief that their differences were too great and allow their past to stand in the way of a happy future? Or would she— please, God—admit that she loved him and invite him to be a part of her life forever?

Lindy snapped another tissue from the box and blew her nose for all she was worth. After several deep breaths and a couple of loud sniffles, she felt certain her crying jag was over.

Travis had commended her on telling Danny the truth, setting him straight, but Lindy felt like a louse, delivering such a harsh blow when her friend was already down for the count. Still, sometimes it was better to take all your lumps at once. That way, when you began building yourself back up, you knew exactly where you stood.

Returning the tissue box to the coffee table, she picked up the framed picture she'd brought downstairs earlier. After Travis had left in Danny's truck, she'd rushed upstairs and changed out of her dirty dress, bypassing her comfy nightshirt collection and opting for Travis's silk shirt instead.

Tonight, they'd connected on an entirely different level. Travis, despite his instinctual need to jump in and single-handedly fix the situation, had yielded to her, recognizing that Danny's heartache was something they had to deal with together.

His respect poked holes in the protective shell she'd built around her heart in a way their budding friendship and exploding passions alone never would have done. Kneeling in the dirt, ferreting out the true reason for Danny's irrational behavior, she'd accepted the fact that she was falling in love with Travis.

Then, as if sealing her fate, when she'd asked to borrow his darn phone, he'd told her he didn't have it, that she was the only one he'd wanted to talk to tonight. Well, that did it. Her heart swelled, shattering its protective shell to bits. Forget falling. She was completely, irrevocably, for ever and ever amen in love with her husband. Again.

"Still," she admitted out loud. Moisture again filled her eyes, but she blinked, refusing to unlock the tears she wasn't sure she'd be able to stop a second time.

Settling back against the couch, she tucked Travis's silk shirt around her thighs and focused on the three young, carefree people in the wedding photo. Danny in his tux, a single red rosebud pinned to his lapel. Barb in a gorgeous Cinderella gown, her thick brown hair tucked under her mother's antique lace veil. Herself in a full-skirted, rose-hued maid-of-honor dress.

Only nine years ago, but the kids in the picture looked so young, so full of hope. She traced Barb's radiant smile with her fingertip. They'd had such grand dreams, but nothing had worked out quite the way they'd planned.

Rufus's wild barking suddenly filled the night air. A few seconds later, she detected the rumble of Danny's truck.

Travis was home.

Heaven help her, she liked the sound of that. Too much.

Enjoy it while you can, because it won't last forever.

Resting the picture against her chest, she dried her cheeks and fluffed her hair. Heavy bootsteps sounded on the porch. She lolled her head on the sofa so she could see into the foyer.

"Hi." She offered Travis a smile as he came through the front door. He looked bone tired. "I thought I might have to come get you."

He stretched his neck from side to side and nudged the door closed behind him. "Danny was unconscious by the time I got him home. Took me a while to get him inside and help Shayna get him into bed." His eyes homed in on her face. "You've been crying."

He rounded the couch in two quick strides and sat beside her, pulling her against his chest, sandwiching the picture frame between them. His wide palm caressed a path down her back, over her hip and back again. The tears she'd been certain were locked up flowed freely once again.

She twined her arm across his stomach, buried her face in his shirt and cried for what seemed like forever. She cried for Barb and Danny, for their precious little girls. She cried for Pops and her parents. She cried for her baby. But mostly, she cried for Travis. For the life she wanted with him, but would never have because neither of them could survive long-term in the other's world.

As her tears fell, Travis held her, his right hand still soothing over her back and hip, his left hand petting her hair. He murmured softly, words of comfort and encouragement, sounds of support. His presence made her feel stronger at her weakest moment. How did he do that?

Two are stronger than one, her conscience insisted.

Yeah, but one was all you can count on.

Lindy cringed at her own cynicism and loosened her grip on Travis. As good as it felt to lean on him during her meltdown, she couldn't let herself become dependent on him. On anyone.

Travis leaned forward to retrieve the tissue box. The frame stabbed him in the ribs. "Ouch," he said, handing her the Kleenex and pulling the picture from between them.

Lindy slouched back against the couch and tried to blow her nose and dry her tears in a more ladylike fashion than before. Travis studied the photograph, a grim twist to his lips.

He tapped the glass under Barb's chin. "So, this is Danny's wife."

"Yeah, that's Barb." Lindy's voice croaked so she cleared her throat, loudly. To heck with ladylike.

"She's beautiful," he said. "Her girls look just like her."

"I know. Some days, I think that's a blessing and some

days, I don't know how Danny and Alice deal with the memories." She tossed her used tissue toward the coffee table.

"You all look so ready to take on the world."

Lindy plucked the photo from his grasp and studied their smiling faces. "We were so young. If only we'd known how devastating it'd be to touch your dreams but not be able to hold on to them."

"Do you think those kids would've done anything differently?" he asked, nodding at the picture. "Would they have skipped the good parts in order to avoid the pain?"

The good parts? Lindy sighed at her own oversight. In her melancholy, she'd overlooked the good things life had given these young people.

All Danny and Barb had ever wanted was to get married, have children and grow old together. Their marriage lasted six blissful years. They created two beautiful daughters to carry on Barb's spirit. Lindy knew without a doubt they both would've sacrificed anything for those girls. Even their dream of growing old together.

And what about her? She'd dreamed of spending a few years in the big city, getting her degree and then moving back to Land's Cross, creating and running Country Daze with the man she loved. She'd done the big city, earned her degree. She'd turned Country Daze into a reality, and for the summer at least, she had the man she loved by her side.

A strong, callused finger tipped her chin up. Travis wiped away a lingering tear drop with his thumb. "A very wise man once told me, 'That which does not kill us makes us stronger,'" he whispered before gently kissing her forehead. The tender gesture touched her heart in a way passion wouldn't have at this moment.

She thought again of those happy people in the photo. "I think you're right. Even if they'd known about the pain, those three kids would have charged forward, anxious to enjoy their happiness, no matter how fleeting."

"They sound like smart people."

"I'm afraid they lost some of that wisdom as they grew up."

"I don't think they lost it. Maybe they just stopped believing in what they knew."

"Yeah, maybe." Head dropped back against the sofa again, she squeezed her eyes shut and rubbed her fingers across the lids then out to massage her temples. "My brain hurts from thinking. I'm completely talked out."

She raised her eyelids and focused on the man beside her. He still looked weary, yet somehow, he appeared invincible. "Would you mind just taking me to bed? I need you to hold me tonight. We can talk tomorrow."

The weariness in his eyes was immediately chased away by the green-and-gold starburst she loved. "Sounds like an excellent plan to me."

Travis held her in his arms, lifting them from the couch as one. As he carried her upstairs, Lindy rested her cheek against his chest, listening to the steady rhythm of his heartbeat.

Right. Right. Right.

The words reverberated through her brain, through her heart, with every beat of Travis's pulse. For the first time in over a year, she began to believe that maybe, together, she and Travis could find a way to make both their dreams come true.

Maybe. It all depended on what happened tomorrow. But was she strong enough to risk her pride and her heart on something as uncertain as the future?

Chapter Fifteen

Sneaking quietly into the barn, Lindy leaned against Louise's stall and studied the gorgeous man squirting fresh milk at Molly and Milton and their kittens. She wanted to capture this moment and remember it forever. This was her dream. A simple life shared with the man she loved.

But Travis's future was not farmwork. Lindy could never live in the city again. So she had to store up her memories now. They'd be all she had to keep her warm for a lifetime of winters.

"Good morning, handsome."

He turned his head, keeping his shoulder butted against Louise as he'd been taught. Dark morning stubble surrounded his sexy grin. "Morning, sweetheart. You look great. As usual."

"Puh-lease. By this time of morning, I'm usually covered in barn muck."

Travis stood, the full milk pail in one hand, the milking stool in the other. "Yeah, but somehow, you make it work."

She giggled at his blatant malarkey and held open the stall gate for him. When Louise turned to follow him, Lindy rubbed a hand between the cow's big brown eyes, stopping her progress.

"Whoa, girl. He's not leaving." Yet, she thought, watching him disappear into the meds room. *He's not leaving us yet.*

Louise butted up against Lindy's palm, stepping as close to the low wall as she could, and turned her head in the direction Travis had disappeared. A low, sad moo erupted from the cow. An answering cry came from the stall next door as Thelma stuck her head over the wall, looking for Travis.

Looks like I'm not the only one mooning over that man. He seems to have claimed all our hearts this summer.

She gave the girls understanding pats to the jaws and followed the object of their affection down the hall. She found him in the bathroom, washing his hands. Walking up behind him, she wrapped her arms around him and hugged, caressing her cheek against his work shirt. "Thanks for handling the chores this morning so I can return Danny's truck."

"No problem. Sure you don't want me to go with you?" His back danced under her cheek as he dried his hands.

"Yeah. He'll be embarrassed enough without an audience."

Travis spun around in her embrace, his arms automatically pulling her tighter against his chest. "Are you sure Dan's gonna want to talk to you this early? I mean, after last night, the man's going to feel like a herd of buffalo are dancing a two-step in his head."

Lindy hid her smile against Travis's chest. Herd of buffalo indeed. At this rate, he wouldn't fit in any better in Atlanta than she had.

"That's all part of my plan. I want to make darned sure he's still suffering when I talk to him. For one thing, that fool got behind the wheel after he'd been drinking. He knows better than that." She burrowed deeper in Travis's warmth, blocking out the remembered sounds of squealing tires and crunching metal.

Travis's arms banded tighter around her. His lips brushed across her head. "I have a feeling after you get through with him, he won't make that mistake again." He pulled back and chucked her under the chin. "If you really want him to suffer, be as loud as possible. Holler, stomp your feet, bang things. Anything that makes noise will be pure torture."

"Oh now, Travis, that's mean. I was thinking about offering him breakfast. A couple of runny eggs, a nice thick, smelly slice of hogshead cheese with a few pickled pig's feet on the side. And of course, a cup of warm beer to wash it all down."

"Wow, lady. That's one wicked nasty streak you've got."

"Don't worry. As long as you stay on my good side," she teased, tapping him on the chest, "you'll be safe."

His hand dropped below her waist, cupping her bottom. "I've seen you from every angle. All your sides look good to me."

Travis lowered his head, joining their smiles, kissing her long and hard. Despite having spent the night wrapped in his arms, when he lifted his head, Lindy's knees were weak. One kiss and she was putty in his hands.

"If you really plan on talking to Robertson this morning, you'd better get going before I find a clean stack of hay somewhere and have my way with you."

"Oh, my. I like the sound of that. Rain check?"

"How long do you expect me to wait?"

"Well, I've already tossed my bike in the back of Danny's truck so I figure I can be back and naked in two hours."

"Make it one," he insisted, nipping her on the neck.

She tilted her head, giving his lips better access to her throat. "It's a five-mile ride back from town. One and a half?"

"Not one second longer," he agreed.

"I promise."

He kissed her again, quickly. "I'll be here waiting for you."

Lindy parked Danny's truck in his empty driveway and killed the engine, climbing down quickly. With her feet again on solid ground, she soothed the nerves fluttering in her stomach. A clatter echoed from the toolshed located off the driveway's right side. Lindy rounded the house to investigate and to her surprise, found a miserable-looking Danny already out of bed.

She stood silently for a moment just inside the shed, watching as he dropped an empty beer bottle in the trash. Clinking glass echoed through the shed. Danny shuddered, his arm taking a swipe at his sweating forehead.

It was easy to imagine how loud that shattering glass must have sounded in Danny's fuzzy, achy head. Lindy searched for some sympathy, but found none.

Fighting to hide her grin, she wondered just how loudly she should demand an explanation for last night's behavior. "Hey, party boy," she began, her voice falsely cheerful and much too loud for a ten-by-twenty aluminum building.

Danny turned bloodshot, hounddog eyes her direction. For a moment, her focus wavered. He looked like he needed a hug, not a kick in the pants. But he'd earned the kick in the pants, and she was here to see he got it. "Where are the girls?"

"Shayna took 'em to Mom's."

"Good. They don't need to witness their dad's downfall."

Danny's scratchy voice interrupted her. "God, Lindy, I'm sorry for being such a jerk last night." He slumped down, half sitting, half leaning on the bumper of his riding mower. "I totally lost it. Not only did I make an ass of myself, but I had no business behind the wheel. I just hope you can forgive me."

"Promise me you'll never do anything that stupid again."

"I swear."

"I forgive you. You forgive me for forgetting?"

"Lindy, you didn't forget. You're moving on. The way Barb would want you to. Want *me* to." His voice hiccuped and when he raised his face to hers, Lindy saw tears swimming in his bloodshot eyes. "You were right about that. Only problem is, I'm still so in love with her, I can't imagine moving on, leaving her behind and starting over with someone else."

"Oh, sweetie, no one expects you to forget Barb. She'll always be a part of you. And the girls. But you do need to look to the future. Somewhere out there is a woman who can love all three of you."

"The idea of falling in love again scares the crap out of me."

"Yeah, me, too." She clasped Danny's hand. "Last night, when Travis got back to the farmhouse, I was crying buckets over a picture of the three of us at y'all's wedding. He asked the most amazing question."

Danny's brows lifted. "What was that?"

"Whether or not I thought those three kids would've changed their futures if they'd known the pain in store for them. You know what I realized?"

"What?"

"Today is all we can control. If we waste time worrying about how the future will turn out, then we'll never have any happiness."

"Wow. When did you get so smart?"

"Right this very second." She grinned into his green face. "I don't know about you, but I'm through letting the heartaches of my past rule my future." She patted Danny's shoulder and stood. "I'm going home to the man I love, and somehow, we're going to figure out a way to make things work."

"Travis must really love you if he's put up with everything we've thrown at him the past two months." Danny grimaced as he stood. "He's a good man, Lindy."

"We decided the same thing about you last night." She tugged on his arm and he automatically bent his knees so she could plant a kiss on his cheek. "You're going to be okay, Danny. Just keep looking forward."

She raced out of the shed and pulled her bicycle out of Danny's truck bed. Childlike joy filled her as she pedaled through town. The future lay before her, and for the first time in ages, she found the idea exciting rather than frightening.

Lindy laughed out loud as she rode past the city limits sign. Three more miles and she'd be home. Anxious to be

on time for her rendezvous with Travis, she pumped her
legs faster, wind whipping her hair around her head.

An hour and twenty-three minutes after leaving Travis
in the barn, Lindy steered off the highway and pedaled
under the Lewis Family Farm archway. Time to change the
sign. Monroe Family Farm had a nice ring to it, she thought
as she coasted down the long driveway.

Halfway to the house, she realized the place felt unnatu-
rally still, lifeless, as if its energy source had been extin-
guished. It was the same stillness she'd felt in the air the
morning of Pops's funeral.

Fighting off that familiar panicky feeling of being left
alone, she rode through the empty spot in the driveway next
to Pops's old truck. She leaned her bike against the porch steps
and looked around. No sign of the silver BMW anywhere.

"He's gone." Her words seem to carry forever in the still
morning air.

Rufus, who was laid out at the top of the porch steps,
raised his head at the sound of her voice. Lindy charged
up the steps, swallowing the bitter bile of fear. She
crouched in front of the old dog. "Did he leave us?"

Droopy brown eyes stared solemnly back at her. The
poor dog looked like he'd been crying. Of course, Rufus
was a bloodhound. He always looked sad.

"No need to panic. Just because he's not here doesn't
mean he's gone." Her words made perfect sense, but they
didn't calm the growing dread coursing through her.
Things had been going too well. Deep down, she'd been
waiting for this moment, unable to fully trust that Travis
would put her first.

She stood and headed for the door, the eerie quiet

ringing in her ears. The screen door squeaked, the way it always did, but the knob refused to turn in her grip. Locked.

"Drat," she whispered, dropping her forehead against the door, losing her grip on what little hope she had left. Not only was she all alone again, she was also locked out of her house.

Think. Don't jump to conclusions. She'd done that too many times, and it always made things worse. Travis wouldn't pack up and leave out of the blue like this. They had plans. And not just rolling-in-the-hay plans.

The open house for Country Daze was this Tuesday, and they'd planned a full-scale sprucing up for the grounds. There was work left to be done, obligations to honor. No, Travis wouldn't just walk away.

"He probably just ran to town." Lindy spun away from the door so quickly the screen door banged shut as she raced back down the porch steps and around the house.

When the back doorknob turned freely in her hand, Lindy felt the urge to sing. She sped through the mudroom and into the kitchen. Noticing a torn sheet of yellow legal paper centered on the table, she skidded to a halt. Her hands trembled as she plucked the note from under the salt and pepper shakers.

Lindy—Julia called. Emergency at home. Grant trouble. Gotta fly to Mexico tonight. Will call later. Sorry. Travis.

Mexico? Lindy balled up the note and heaved it across the room. If Travis was going to Mexico, then it was all over. No way he could get there, deal with whatever mess Grant had created this time and get back in less than two days. He'd spent two nights in Atlanta last week. According to the terms of the will, he could only be away one more night this month.

Once again, he'd put her last, and it was going to cost her everything. She'd lose the farm and Country Daze, all her dreams. And she'd lose her memories, the ones she'd planned to make with Travis to keep her company after he left.

She'd known losing Travis a second time would be painful, but it wasn't supposed to happen so soon. They were supposed to have the whole summer to build memories. She was supposed to have enough time to prepare herself for this moment.

But she wasn't prepared. Travis's desertion had blindsided her. He'd lulled her into depending on him again.

"I'm such an idiot." Lindy plodded across the kitchen and kicked the yellow paper ball toward the hall. "How could I let him do this to me? *Again.*"

She took another whack at the wadded note, then another, kicking it down the hall, into the study. The paper silently collided with Pops's sturdy oak desk. She wished there'd been a loud thunk, something to give voice to her rising anger.

The anger felt good, comfortable. Lately she'd spent too much time crying. Those days were over. "Time to take charge."

Rummaging through the desk looking for a clean pad of paper, Lindy slammed the drawers, filling the room with satisfying thunks. "By God, if anyone's going to nullify this will it's going to be me. Let him rush off to Grant's rescue. Who needs him?"

Trying to tune out the shouts of "You do!" resonating from the recesses of her cracked heart, Lindy continued her paper search. She needed to draft a letter to Chester right away, calling an end to this farce before Travis defaulted on their agreement. Her pride demanded she end it first.

She yanked open the bottom right-hand drawer and found a dozen lined, yellow legal tablets. Pretty certain she'd never again write on anything but plain white paper, she slammed the drawer shut and headed upstairs.

Travis was bound to have plenty of white paper in his room. She liked the idea of using Monroe Enterprises office supplies to write her kiss-off letter.

When she threw open the door to Travis's room, his familiar scent assailed her, stealing her breath like a sucker punch to the gut. Against her will, her eyes strayed to his bed. The jeans and shirt he'd worn this morning when she and the cows had mooned over him—was that really just this morning?—lay crosswise over the blue comforter.

He'd obviously left in a hurry. Normally a tidy man, Travis wouldn't have left dirty clothes on his bed otherwise.

Of course he'd left in a hurry. The note said emergency, didn't it? But with Grant, everything was an emergency.

Maybe this time was different. Suddenly her anger was tempered by concern. And shame. From the moment she'd read his note, the only person she'd thought about was herself.

What if Grant were sick? People got strange illnesses in Mexico all the time, didn't they? Oh, no, she thought, sliding into the straight-back aluminum chair Alice had provided as Travis's desk chair. What if Grant was seriously hurt? Or dead?

"Oh, Travis. Please forgive me." He wasn't the one repeating past mistakes. It was her. Jumping to conclusions. Running off in a huff rather than standing up for what she wanted.

And she wanted Travis.

He'd obviously gotten bad news this morning and

rushed off to be with his family. He hadn't abandoned her, he hadn't chosen them over her. He'd simply prioritized his commitments. The same way she'd done last night when she'd postponed her making-love-under-the-stars fantasy in order to deal with the immediacy of Danny's drunkenness.

A vile mixture of shame and queasiness rolled through her stomach. Had she always been this selfish?

She needed to find a number for someone in Atlanta, someone who could fill her in. Travis's family needed his support, and he needed hers.

Just like she needed his.

Husband and wife. For better or worse. Till death do us part. She'd sworn the oath, but until now, she'd done a lousy job of upholding her end of the deal. Hopefully it wasn't too late to change that. To hell with their different backgrounds and lifestyles.

Lindy wanted a life with Travis. That was the only dream that mattered. She was going to stand by her husband through this crisis. Afterward, she would do her darnedest to convince Travis they could make it work somehow. If they could turn a heap of old boards into a beautiful pavilion, then together, they could accomplish whatever they set their minds to.

Her heart pumped like she'd mainlined caffeine as she hunted for contact information. Lindy had never even bothered to write down his blasted cell phone number. She needed to talk to his secretary. Marge would know what was going on and how to locate Travis.

Lindy unearthed a notepad and recognized it as the one Travis was scribbling on the day she'd overheard his conversation with Julia. The day he'd told her how much his marriage vows meant. She could kick herself for being too stubborn to hear what he'd been trying to tell her that day.

With trembling fingers, she flipped open the notepad cover and read the bold words scrawled across the top of the first page. *Lindy's birthday.*

"Oh, my," she whispered, her fingers fluttering over the pictures, tracing the objects he'd drawn. The top page showed a child-size version of a teeter-totter, made from grayed barn wood balanced on old-fashioned milk cans. He'd colored the cans pumpkin-orange, Country Daze's signature color.

She turned to the second page, where he'd drawn a miniature red barn with a slide coming out of the hayloft, landing a laughing child into a mound of straw. Off to the side, he'd sketched in the tractor-tire swings Lindy had already hung.

Her fingers paused over the little girl he'd drawn sliding out of the hayloft. She had curly blond hair, bright green eyes and an enormous smile.

Tears filled her eyes as she clutched the papers to her breast. He'd captured her vision perfectly, filling in little details she hadn't even mentioned. *This* was the new project he'd just undertaken. The one he wasn't certain would work out.

He planned on giving her a playground for her birthday. The implication of his gift sunk in. Travis wanted to invest himself in her dream. By building her this playground, he'd add his own unique touch to Country Daze.

Did that mean he wanted to stay in Tennessee and build a life with her? Or did he want her to have something to remember him by after he left?

Laying the notepad back on the desk, she flipped it back to the laughing little girl. This was the real gift. Travis wanted to offer her a home, a family. A true marriage. She wouldn't let a little thing like geography stand in the way.

As Travis drove south, he tried not to think about how hurt Lindy would be by his quick disappearance. He noted the time on the dashboard clock. She'd promised to be home in another half an hour. He should be waiting for her in a bed of fresh hay, searching for the right words to convince her to trust in their future.

He should *not* be rushing to Atlanta on a moment's notice.

His knuckles had gone white against the steering wheel, so Travis loosened his grip. He'd wait another thirty minutes, then call the farm and try to explain the situation to Lindy.

Julia's phone call had been frantic, her words barely a whisper. "Grant's in jail. In Mexico."

Discovering Grant was back in Mexico was bad enough, but prison? This was by far the worst mess of Grant's life. Travis had had to leave Land's Cross immediately. He had no choice. His mother would've expected him to fix this problem.

He'd wanted to hang up, to ignore Julia's news, but of course, he couldn't do that. Instead he'd asked, "What the hell did he do?"

"He ran up some gambling debts he can't pay. Your father received a registered letter from a Mexican attorney saying Grant wouldn't be released from prison until someone makes restitution."

"Can't you just wire the money?"

"No. This time the casino owner threatened to sue unless

someone goes down there, pays up and personally escorts Grant out of the country." She sighed dramatically. "You're the only one who can fix this, Travis."

He slammed his fist against the center console. *You're the only one who can fix this, Travis.* How many times had he heard that in his lifetime? And every time, without fail, he dropped whatever he was doing and charged to the rescue.

Snaking his left hand through his hair, Travis squinted into the distance and caught sight of a familiar red and white real estate sign. Did it always have to be him? Why was he the only one who could fix things?

As he approached, the defunct Holcombe County Co-op warehouse came into view. Tapping his brake, Travis disengaged the cruise control and pulled over onto the shoulder, rolling to stop in front of the old building. Thanks to Brad Middleton's excellent legal investigation skills, Travis would soon be the proud new owner of this property.

You're the only one who can fix this.

Julia's words ricocheted around his brain, taunting him. He jumped out of the car. What if he didn't want to drop what he was doing this time and charge to Grant's rescue? What if he called his father and told the old man he wouldn't do it?

"He'd find someone else to fix it." His own words floated back to him on the breeze, and Travis realized it was the truth. If he didn't step in and deal with this problem, Winston would hire someone.

"It doesn't have to be me." Travis felt the burden he'd carried for fifteen years lift from his shoulders as he released himself from the promise he'd made his mother. He'd done all he could to look out for Grant and Winston. Now it was time to look out for Travis. And Lindy.

Lindy, the woman he loved, the woman he wanted to spend the rest of his life with, the one person who really, truly, needed him. He was the only person who could help save her farm and make her dreams come true. And that need was not an obligation he was duty-bound to honor.

No, she kept Travis centered, directed his focus onto what truly mattered in life: friends who loved you like family, satisfaction from hard work done well. Peace. Happiness.

He took another look at the empty warehouse. At some point during the past few weeks, the ideal solution for this property had finally occurred to him. All across the south, rural farming communities were reinventing themselves. Tourist destinations. Retirement communities. Commerce centers. Those formerly repressed areas were unilaterally in need of affordable housing.

When he looked at this worn-down building, he could see a new apartment building as easily as Lindy saw a picnic pavilion in a pile of old barn wood. Standing on the side of a rural Tennessee highway in the bright light of midmorning, Travis realized his dream of branching off from Monroe Enterprises was no longer just a vague plan. With this warehouse project, he could—and would—have his independence.

Travis took a last look at the warehouse and knew he wouldn't be rushing to Atlanta today. He was already late for a date with his wife. Turning back to his car, he plucked the phone from his hip so he could call his father and let him know someone else would have to deal with Grant's problems today.

Over the silver hood of his car, he noticed an auto dealership across the street. White banners with the word *Truck* written in blue flapped from the light poles. An idea took shape in the back of Travis's mind as he spoke to his father, recommending an attorney for Grant, relinquishing his day-to-day responsibility for the other two Monroe men and resigning from his position as president of Monroe Enterprises.

When the old man quit yelling, Travis said firmly, "I'm not resigning from the family, Dad. It's time I started a family and a business of my own. If Grant doesn't want my old job, you've got a dozen well-qualified people already on the payroll. Promote one of them. I'm staying in Tennessee. With Lindy."

Feeling liberated, he turned his cell phone off and U-turned across the highway, directly into the dealership parking lot. He had one more piece of business to take care of before going home to his wife.

Lindy had been unable to locate a phone number for Travis's secretary, which made perfect sense. He surely had her numbers memorized, or more likely, programmed into speed dial. And since it was Saturday, Lindy doubted she'd find the woman at the office anyway.

So, she did the next best thing. She packed a suitcase and asked Alice to look out for the place while she was gone.

"Where in the world are you going?" Alice had asked.

"Atlanta. My husband needs me."

"Well, good for you. Drive safe."

Lindy gripped the steering wheel of Pops's old truck and chuckled under her breath. Alice didn't even question the notion of Lindy chasing off after Travis. She'd even volunteered to give Shayna a call and make arrangements for the open house on Tuesday. Chances were Lindy wouldn't make it back in time.

"If you don't get a move on, you'll still be sitting in the driveway on Tuesday." She turned the ignition and slowly reversed out of the parking area. Despite her recent success driving Travis's car to the mailbox and back, Lindy was still nervous about tackling the open road.

Puttering around Land's Cross, with its two stop signs and single traffic light, was one thing. But six hours of solitary highway followed by the chaos of Atlanta traffic was another thing altogether.

"Quit borrowing trouble," she fussed. "One step at a time. First, just get yourself to the end of the driveway." She put the old truck in gear and lurched forward. A single bead of sweat trickled down her back. She settled more comfortably in the seat, exhaling on a huff.

Concentrate on Travis. Imagine the look on his face when you tell him you love him.

She reached the end of the driveway and inhaled deeply. "Next step, pull out on the highway."

Glancing both directions, she noticed a shiny red pickup truck coming in her direction in the northbound lane. She wiped her palms against her thighs as she waited for the driver to pass.

The truck's blinker flipped on, indicating a right-hand turn, which would lead the other driver into her driveway. As the vehicle drew nearer, she noticed the remnants of white shoe polish numbers on the windshield.

What rotten timing. Someone was coming out to show off their new truck, but she didn't have time for company. She had to catch up with Travis.

Lindy cranked down the window, prepared to offer her visitor a quick congrats and send them on their way. When the truck pulled into the driveway, Travis sat behind the wheel.

Lindy wrinkled her brow. Wasn't he supposed to be halfway to Atlanta by now?

He lowered his window, and they spoke at the same time.

"Where are you going?" he asked.

"Why aren't you in Atlanta? Is Grant okay?"

"Nothing a lawyer and my father's checkbook can't cure."

"So he's not hurt? Sick?"

"No."

They stared at each other for a second, then both spoke again.

"Atlanta," she answered.

"I changed my—" He paused and Lindy could see her answer sinking into his brain. "You're going to Atlanta?" he asked.

She propped her elbow on the windowsill and planted her chin in her palm. "Yep."

His fingers tunneled through his already disheveled hair. "I think we need to talk."

"I think you're right." She wanted to lean out her window and kiss that confused little furrow between his brows. "I like your new truck."

His head shook slightly. "What?" he asked, obviously confused by her abrupt change of subject.

"Your new truck? I like it."

"Oh, thanks." And then, as if suddenly picking up on her happiness vibe, he smiled. "Want to go for a ride?"

"I thought you'd never ask." She killed her truck's engine. "Where to?"

Travis nodded down the driveway. "How about a ride home?"

Home. God that sounded good. "I'd like that. Very much." She hopped out of the old truck, leaving it right in the middle of the driveway, and rounded the front of Travis's new truck. Standing at the passenger door, she felt a familiar wave of weak-kneed fear.

She glanced through the window and saw Travis's encouraging smile. Determinedly beating back her nerves, she grasped the handle and opened the door. As she climbed in, she caught a whiff of new car, but mostly, she smelled cedar and sea breeze.

"I knew you could do it," Travis whispered as she settled in the passenger seat. He took her hand. "Ready?"

Lindy sucked her lower lip between her teeth and met his smiling gaze. "Ready," she said, nodding. Her hand squeezed his in a death grip.

Travis rolled slowly down the long driveway, his thumb caressing the back of her hand. Lindy's heart beat frantically the entire time, but it had very little to do with the ride. She felt anything but powerless sitting on Travis's right-hand side.

In fact, she felt powerful. Her future, her happily-ever-after, was within her grasp. And with Travis by her side, what did she have to fear?

Travis pulled into his usual parking spot and put the truck in Park, killed the engine. Then he hauled her across the bench seat and into his lap, squeezing her so tight she could feel the buttons of his shirt pressing against her skin.

"You did it, sweetheart! You did it."

She tilted her head back and looked up at him. "We did it, Travis. We did it."

"I guess we did." He lowered his lips toward hers, then suddenly pulled back. His eyes were dark and serious. "I think we should talk first."

She nodded silently. He let her go and climbed out of the truck. She slid under the steering wheel and slipped her right hand into his, allowing him to help her down. Fingers linked, they climbed the porch steps and sat on the swing.

"Were you really planning on driving to Atlanta?"

"Yes."

"Why?"

"Because I love you, Travis, and I want to be with you. Wherever you are will always be my home."

"Lindy." Travis leaned down to kiss her, but she wasn't finished. She pulled back a fraction. He instantly sat straighter, a hurt and confused look on his face.

"There's more," she said, taking a deep breath and reaching into her back pocket. Grasping his left hand in hers she slid from the swing and knelt on the porch. The hard wood bit into her knees, reminding her this was real.

She turned his hand up and dropped her wedding ring into his open palm. When she looked up at him, the green-and-gold starburst shimmered through tears. His tears, this time.

"Travis Monroe, you are the most vital element in all my dreams. I want to be your wife again. I want to have babies with you. Grow old together. And I've been thinking, Country Daze would probably be more of a success in a metropolitan area like Atlanta. Either way, Atlanta or Land's Cross, it doesn't matter, as long as we stay together. Forever."

Lindy rested her hands on his knees and waited for his response. When he tossed his head back and laughed, her heart stopped beating. When he slid off the swing and knelt in front of her, it started racing so fast she feared she might pass out.

He picked up her limp left hand and slid the diamond solitaire on her third finger. "Lindy, you've always been my wife. Distance never could change that. Never will." He lifted her hand, splaying it across his chest, her wedding ring resting over his heart. "Sweetheart, I hope you won't be disappointed, but I don't even want to consider living in Atlanta. My home's here, in Land's Cross, with you."

"But what about your father and the family business?"

"I quit Monroe Enterprises this morning. I also resigned from my position as family problem solver. Grant and my father are in charge of their own lives."

"What will you do now?"

"You know that old abandoned warehouse about forty-five miles south of here on Highway 411?"

"The old co-op?" Why the heck was he talking about an old warehouse? She just professed her undying love for God's sake.

"Yep. That old building is slated to become the first renovation project for L&M Construction."

"L&M Construction?"

"You see, I realized that depressed farming communities needed revitalization projects just as badly as urban areas. Turning the old co-op into an apartment complex will be Lewis and Monroe Construction's inaugural project."

"Lewis and Monroe Construction?" Lindy asked, afraid to believe what she was hearing.

"Well, it's just a suggestion. If you don't like it, we can come up with something different."

"You want us to form a construction company together?"

"Lindy, I want us to do everything together, for the rest of our lives."

"You do?"

"Definitely. You've taught me how important it is to chase your dreams, and I've realized that my dream, aside from running the most successful construction company Tennessee has ever seen, is to be a husband. And a part-time farmer. And, God willing, a father. Any idea where a guy might find a job like that around here?"

"I might. What are your qualifications?"

"Let me show you," Travis whispered, pressing his lips against hers.

Lindy wrapped her arms around the man of her dreams. Travis cupped her head in his big, strong hand and lowered her to the porch floor. Breaking the kiss, he framed her face in his hands, that beloved green-gold starburst shining in his eyes.

"Lindy Lewis Monroe, I love you." He dropped another kiss on her lips and she attempted to capture him, but he pulled away too quickly. "Will you marry me?"

"Again?"

"Sweetheart, with you, once is never enough."

This time, when she reached for him, he didn't resist. She wrapped both arms tightly around her husband and glued her lips to his.

Finally, it all felt right—the blissful weight of her wedding ring snug on her finger, the tingling pleasure of Travis in her arms, the pending success of Country Daze and,

most importantly, the exciting discovery that the man she
loved most in the world was hers to keep. Forever.

To have and to hold, from this day forward.

Thanks, Pops.

* * * * *

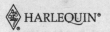

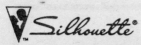

COMING NEXT MONTH

SPECIAL EDITION

#1861 A FAMILY FOR THE HOLIDAYS—Victoria Pade
Montana Mavericks: Striking It Rich
Widow Shandie Solomon moved to Montana with her infant daughter for a new lease on life—and got one, when she opened her beauty parlor next door to Dex Traub's motorcycle shop. By Christmastime the bad boy of Thunder Canyon had Shandie hooked…and she couldn't tell if it was sleigh bells or wedding bells ringing in her future.

#1862 THE SHEIK AND THE CHRISTMAS BRIDE—
Susan Mallery
Desert Rogues
Prince As'ad of El Deharia agreed to adopt three orphaned American girls on one condition—that their teacher Kayleen James take over as nanny. In a heartbeat the young ladies turned the playboy prince's household upside down…and Kayleen turned his head. Now he would do anything to keep her—and make her his Christmas bride!

#1863 CAPTURING THE MILLIONAIRE—Marie Ferrarella
The Sons of Lily Moreau
It was a dark and stormy night…when lawyer Alain Dulac crashed his BMW into a tree, and local veterinarian Kayla McKenna came to his aid. Used to rescuing dogs and cats, Kayla didn't know what to make of this strange new animal—but his magnetism was undeniable. Did she have what it took to add this inveterate bachelor to her menagerie?

#1864 DEAR SANTA—Karen Templeton
Guys and Daughters
Investment guru Grant Braeburn had his hands full juggling stock portfolios and his feisty four-year-old daughter, Haley. So the distant widower reluctantly turned to his former wife's flighty best friend Mia Vaccaro for help. Soon Haley's Christmas list included marriage between her daddy and Mia. But would Santa deliver the goods?

#1865 THE PRINCESS AND THE COWBOY—Lois Faye Dyer
The Hunt for Cinderella
Before rancher Justin Hunt settled for a marriage of convenience that would entitle him to inherit a fortune, he went to see the estranged love of his life, Lily Spencer, one more time—and discovered he was a father. Could the owner of Princess Lily's Lingerie and the superrich cowboy overcome their volatile emotions and make love work this time?

#1866 DÉJÀ YOU—Lynda Sandoval
Return to Troublesome Gulch
When a fatal apartment blaze had firefighter Erin DeLuca seeing red over memories of her prom-night car accident that took her fiancé and unborn child years ago, ironically, it was pyrotechnics engineer Nate Walker who comforted her. At least for one night. Now, if only they could make the fireworks last longer…

SSECNM1007